THE DANGEROUS DAMES

Selina—a sultry slave girl who was top prize in a poker game . . . winner take all

Leila—a blonde belly dancer, just a shade too thin for her profession

Beatrice—a mountainous woman with a taste for lithe young men

Kitty—a healthy young seductress who was fetching in leopard-print lingerie . . . fatal without

Danny Boyd always enjoyed games with dames, but this time he was in a race to recover some hot diamonds—with a crew of killers at his heels. And it was much too dangerous to dally. Especially when someone had plans for the hardworking detective, plans that began with houris and ended with homicide.

SIGNET Thrillers

by *Carter Brown*

Angel (#S2094—35¢)
The Blonde (#S1972—35¢)
The Bombshell (#1767—25¢)
The Brazen (#S1836—35¢)
The Corpse (#1606—25¢)
The Dame (#1738—25¢)
The Desired (#1764—25¢)
The Dream is Deadly
  (#S1845—35¢)
The Dumdum Murder
  (#S2196—35¢)
The Ever-Loving Blues
  (#S1919—35¢)
The Exotic (#S2009—35¢)
The Girl Who Was Possessed
  (#G2291—40¢)
Graves, I Dig! (#S1801—35¢)
The Guilt-Edged Cage
  (#S2220—35¢)
The Hellcat (#S2122—35¢)
The Hong Kong Caper
  (#S2180—35¢)
The Ice-Cold Nude
  (#S2110—35¢)
The Lady Is Transparent
  (#S2148—35¢)
Lament for a Lousy Lover
  (#S1856—35¢)
The Lover (#1620—25¢)
Lover, Don't Come Back
  (#S2183—35¢)
The Loving and the Dead
  (#1654—25¢)
The Million Dollar Babe
  (#S1909—35¢)

The Mistress (#1594—25¢)
Murder in the Key Club
  (#S2140—35¢)
Murder Wears a Mantilla
  (#S2048—35¢)
A Murderer Among Us
  (#S2228—35¢)
The Myopic Mermaid
  (#S1924—35¢)
The Passionate Pagan
  (#S2259—35¢)
The Sad-Eyed Seductress
  (#S2023—35¢)
The Savage Salome
  (#S1896—35¢)
The Stripper (#S1981—35¢)
The Temptress (#S1817—35¢)
Terror Comes Creeping
  (#1750—25¢)
The Tigress
  (#S1989—35¢)
Tomorrow Is Murder
  (#S1806—35¢)
The Unorthodox Corpse
  (#S1950—35¢)
The Victim (#1633—25¢)
Walk Softly, Witch
  (#1663—25¢)
The Wanton (#1713—25¢)
The Wayward Wahine
  (#1784—25¢)
The White Bikini
  (#S2275—35¢)
Zelda (#S2033—35¢)

TO OUR READERS: If your dealer does not have the SIGNET and MENTOR books you want, you may order them by mail, enclosing the list price plus 5¢ a copy to cover mailing. If you would like our free catalog, please request it by postcard. The New American Library of World Literature, Inc., P. O. Box 2310, Grand Central Station, New York 17, New York.

the *carter brown*
mystery series

nymph to the slaughter

A SIGNET BOOK

published by
**THE NEW AMERICAN LIBRARY
OF WORLD LITERATURE, INC.**

in association with
HORWITZ PUBLICATIONS INC.

© Copyright 1963 by Horwitz Publications Inc. Pty. Ltd., Sydney, Australia. Reproduction in part or in whole in any language expressly forbidden in any part of the world without the written consent of Horwitz Publications Inc. Pty. Ltd.

All rights reserved

Published by arrangement with Alan G. Yates

FIRST PRINTING, JUNE, 1963

SIGNET TRADEMARK REG. U.S. PAT. OFF. AND FOREIGN COUNTRIES
REGISTERED TRADEMARK—MARCA REGISTRADA
HECHO EN CHICAGO, U.S.A.

SIGNET BOOKS are published by
The New American Library of World Literature, Inc.
501 Madison Avenue, New York 22, New York

PRINTED IN THE UNITED STATES OF AMERICA

nymph to the slaughter

chapter 1

So anything can happen in Manhattan during the middle of a July heat wave but when a near-naked slave girl—straight out of the Arabian Nights—appeared in the doorway of a Sutton Place penthouse at five-thirty in the afternoon, I figured the whole thing just had to be ridiculous. Either it was sunstroke, or I should be on my way to Bellevue wrapped real tight in a restrainer.

"Yeah?" The mirage had a listless voice.

I closed my eyes and whimpered a little.

"You sound like the heat got to you already," she said with morbid interest. "With the crew cut you should wear a hat, but always."

I opened my eyes again reluctantly. She was still there, one bare shoulder propped against the doorjamb, her wide brown eyes examining my face dispassionately. Her thick black hair tumbled down to her shoulders with magnificent disdain, like she forgot to put it up a couple of days back and the hell with it now. The inadequate red satin vest only just buttoned across the front of her wondrously full breasts, and from there on down to her hips was an unnerving expanse of naked olive-tanned skin. The baggy silk pants were semiopaque, gathered at the ankles with outsize brass bangles, while she walked around barefoot like the original Salome. It *had* to be the heat.

"My name's Boyd," I mumbled at her, "Danny Boyd. I came to see a guy called Osman Bey, but I guess I picked the wrong fantasy, or something."

"You've come to the right place," she said encouragingly.

"Maybe he's busy?" I suggested. "I could come back in the fall when it's cooler."

"He's only fooling around with his hooker," she said, smiling. "Come right on in, Mr. Boyd."

"I guess I'll come back later when he's all through fooling around with his hooker," I gulped, "like when she's gone and all."

"Hook-*ah*!" she snapped. "Not hook-er! It's a thing for smoking, not—well!—all I can say is some people have dirty minds!"

"Maybe I should just go now and never come back?" I pleaded with her.

"You'd better come in," she said with a sniff, "and this is just my working outfit so keep your mind to yourself, huh?"

I followed the awe-inspiring bounce of her silk-clad rear end into the apartment. With each successive step I took, the air grew heavier with an aromatic flavor, like someone was burning incense.

The living room looked about as American as the slave girl did. A beautiful white sheepskin rug covered the floor, and plush jumbo-sized cushions were scattered carelessly across it—so who needed a chair? For sure, the guy sitting cross-legged on a plum-colored velvet cushion didn't, because he had his hookah for company. It was the first time I'd seen one of those weird gismos outside a comic strip, and it was fascinating in a repulsive kind of way. I couldn't see the detail too well because all the shades were drawn tight and everything was draped in semigloom. But every time the guy sucked smoke through the water, the

NYMPH TO THE SLAUGHTER

hookah made a gurgling sound that was halfway obscene.

"This is Danny Boyd," the slave girl announced glumly. "He looks like a no-good dirty-minded fink to me, but I guess that's your problem, huh?"

"Are you Osman Bey?" I asked the guy in a real curious voice.

He stroked the tuft of beard that hung from his chin like an afterthought with the glue peeling, and faint interest showed in his dark eyes.

"Please sit down, Mr. Boyd." He gestured toward one of the jumbo-sized cushions.

I sat down awkwardly and waited while he took another puff on his hookah; it took a hell of a long time before the smoke finally got around to his mouth, and I had plenty of opportunity to look him over.

His long black hair was thick and oily; his skin swarthy and smooth across the fat cheeks. He wore a blue silk shirt over his bulging paunch and a pair of shapeless bilious-green pants that fit tight over his thighs. The bare feet were long and dainty like a woman's, the toenails lacquered silver. Mostly, he looked like an unnamed disease.

"I am Osman Bey!" he announced with a puff of scented smoke, like it was a revelation. "Welcome to my house."

"Thanks a bunch!" I growled.

"Selina!" He clapped his hands together sharply. "We will have coffee."

"So big deal!" the slave girl sneered. Then she bounced gently out of the room, and the rear view looked like a couple of king-sized balloons ricocheting against each other the whole time.

My curiosity twitched so bad I couldn't take it any more. "Selina—uh—she's your wife?" I queried, trying hard to sound like I was only making polite conversation.

Osman Bey shuddered, then made a derogatory sound deep in his throat. "You jest, my friend? I got her in payment of a bad debt."

"She didn't mind being used as a pay-off?"

"For Selina, anything is better than working for a living," he said obliquely. "In my own country, in the good old days I would have given her the bastinado two or three times a day to see if that would cure her sloth!"

"Bastinado?"

"Beat the soles of her feet with a pliant cane," he explained in a dreamy voice. "Don't you agree that we've all become overcivilized?"

Selina returned carrying a tray, and served coffee in a demitasse to each of us. I took a long sip without thinking and wound up with a mouthful of bitter-tasting mud. Within a couple of seconds a wave of nausea swept over me as my stomach dared my throat to actually swallow the garbage.

"Ah!" Osman Bey smacked his lips appreciatively. "Turkish coffee is the only coffee."

"With pastrami on rye it's real great," Selina added, then watched my face with morbid satisfaction.

My throat reacted in a convulsive swallow, then my stomach called a mass indignation meeting someplace high in my chest.

Osman Bey put down his empty cup and gazed at me steadily with a deep melancholy showing in his dark eyes. The over-all effect was like someone had firmly pressed a couple of olive pits into an overripe avocado pear. It didn't help my stomach at all.

"Now to business, my friend," he said sadly. "My life is ruined. I am shamed, dishonored, and reviled, unless you can help me!"

"You could try instant coffee for a start?" I suggested helpfully.

"This is no time for jokes," he said, sighing deeply. "My partner and lifelong friend, Abdul Murad, sent me his greatest possession—trusting in Allah and myself that no harm could come of it—and I have betrayed him." For a moment he looked like he was about to burst into tears. "I rely on your skill and talent, my friend, to retrieve this treasure before my

NYMPH TO THE SLAUGHTER

friend and partner has the chance to discover it is missing."

"What kind of treasure, exactly?" I asked.

"His daughter Marta," he whimpered. "A jewel of a girl and his only progeny; without her his life means nothing!" Osman Bey shuddered. "And if he ever discovers she is missing, my life will also mean nothing. In fury, Abdul Murad is a terrible man—a direct descendant of the Ottomans who ruled by the sword! If he finds out his daughter is lost my life would not be worth that much!" He snapped his fingers dramatically.

"How come you lost her in the first place?"

"She arrived by airplane, went to her hotel, then called me and said she would be here within the hour," he said in a dismal voice. "I waited, joyous and expectant, to welcome my partner and lifelong friend's dearest and only daughter to my humble house. She did not come. I called the hotel and they told me she had checked out a half-hour before without leaving any forwarding address. Two men had visited with her, and she left with them."

His dark eyes looked about to dissolve entirely. "There is only one possible answer, my friend. Marta Murad was kidnaped!"

"It happened this morning?" I queried.

"Four days back," he said. "Ninety-six hours of torture and torment I have already endured."

"The police can't find her?"

"Among the teeming spires and minarets of Manhattan," he said very carefully, "one young girl can be lost forever."

"You mean you haven't called the police in at all?" I grunted.

"I need an even greater efficiency—yourself, my good friend." He smiled hopefully. "I hear of your reputation—D. Boyd, the smartest private detective alive! For the daughter of my old friend and partner I must have nothing less than the best."

"It took you four whole days to figure that out?" I asked in a wondering voice.

"I hoped she would call, maybe something had happened to explain her absence rationally." He smiled again, and the honeydew that beaded his top lip had nothing to do with passion. "But finally I realized she was not going to call and somehow I had to find her. That is why I called the greatest private detective in New York to entrust him with the task."

"She came into the country legally?" I asked.

"But, of course!" His eyes expressed horror at the thought of any illegality. "As a tourist with the proper visa—just to visit with her father's partner for a few weeks."

"What did she bring in with her?"

He caressed that depressing tuft of beard for a few seconds, then finally shrugged. "So smart! I picked the right man in D. Boyd, I can see that already. Yes, she did bring something with her, a small present from my partner, a token of his esteem and affection for me. A sober and solemn gift that indicated the spiritual and moral values of our partnership that has endured so long. Something rare and valuable indeed, D. Boyd, a genuine first edition of Yusuf Kamil Pasha's translation of Racine's *Fénelon*.

"Oh, really?" I said blankly.

"It is a very rare book indeed!"

"Maybe four ounces of heroin glued inside the binding made it even rarer?" I suggested politely.

"Heroin?" His cheeks quivered with righteous indignation. "Those filthy drugs? I would not defile my soul by—"

"Then what?" I grated.

Osman Bey shrugged massively, then gave me a nervous, confiding grin. "Well, maybe just a few little diamonds, D. Boyd? Those you would have no objection to, I am sure?"

"Exactly how few of those diamonds I don't object to, did Marta Murad have hidden in that rare first edition?" I asked coldly.

"The actual number of stones I can only guess," he said apologetically. "Their value I would estimate at somewhere close to, say, two hundred thousand dollars?"

"So she was kidnaped and they knew what they were after," I said bleakly. "They knew you wouldn't dare call the cops because of the smuggled diamonds. I wouldn't want to bet on what's happened to the girl during the last four days, but I'll bet on what's happened to those diamonds for sure."

"A man places his trust in Allah and lives in hope," Osman said with mock piety. "I will pay you to find the diamonds for me, D. Boyd, and the girl of course!" The bit about the girl sounded like an afterthought. "If you succeed or fail, it is kismet! You can only try—no man can do more."

"He can do a hell of a lot less," I growled.

"For—" he closed his eyes and thought hard for a few seconds "—five thousand dollars now, and ten thousand more if you find the diamonds and return them to me—with the girl also—a man like you, D. Boyd, would do his best, right?"

"Right," I said quickly before he changed his mind.

"Selina!" He snapped his fingers imperiously. "Bring the money."

The slave girl came back a short time later and handed me a thick envelope. I opened it and carefully counted the crisp hundred-dollar bills inside. There were fifty exactly.

"The hotel won't give me a lead," I told him. "You want me to do the kind of job the cops can do a hundred times better, and quicker, like checking the hospitals, the morgue, the whole routine?"

"I do not think my worthy partner and lifelong friend's only daughter is either sick or dead," he said flatly. "I think she is only kidnaped as I told you before, you remember? Kidnaped to discourage me from seeking the return of my diamonds. When they have disposed of them, I think they will no longer have any use for Marta Murad so they will set her free. You have to find her before that happens, D. Boyd, and then you will also find my diamonds."

"Okay," I said. "But you still haven't given me any kind of a lead. Who knew the diamonds were hidden in the bookbinding, anyway? Your partner, Abdul Murad, did because he sent them—and you knew they were on their way with his daughter. Who else knew so much they could organize the kidnaping of the girl and the stones within a couple of hours after she arrived in New York?"

Osman Bey gave me a long sorrowful look. "Mohammed once said, 'Verily the best of women are those who are content with a little.' I have yet to find one, D. Boyd! I have a—uh—weakness for belly dancers, you understand? One in particular I met a few months back and we established what you would call a relationship. I confided some of my secrets to her, and I feel now my trust was badly misplaced. Her name is Leila Zenta."

"I suppose you've confronted her with this in the last day or so—right?"

Bey shrugged elaborately. "Why would I do that? If she has betrayed me, would she tell me? No, I have not talked to her. But you might."

"Where do I find her?"

"She works at a place called the Ottoman Club."

"Nobody else you can think of?" I queried.

He shook his head firmly. "Nobody. It has to be Leila, my friend."

"I'll go talk with her tonight," I promised, "and report back to you in the morning."

There was that slow, bubbling, faintly obscene sound again as he took a long puff on his hookah. "I think," he said finally, "I would rather call you sometime tomorrow for your report, D. Boyd."

"Have it your way," I said, shrugging.

"Selina will escort you to the door." He stroked his tuft of beard with infinite gentleness. "I wish you every success. May Allah go with you."

"To see a belly dancer?"

"If Allah in his infinite wisdom first created the bel-

NYMPH TO THE SLAUGHTER 15

ly," he said gently, "then the dance dedicated to it is merely a matter of paying homage, is it not?"

"You should have been a lawyer," I told him in an admiring voice.

"I should have been tight-lipped in the company of my favorite weakness," he said bleakly. "Then I would not be worried about my partner's daughter or the valuable diamonds I have lost!"

It was a thought to take with me to the front hall. The slave girl opened the door for me, then gave a deep sigh. What it did to that inadequate red satin vest would have confused an anatomy student. I turned my head a fraction so she got the perfection of my left profile full blast.

"Don't tell me you got troubles, too?" I said in a sympathetic voice.

"A belly dancer he wants," she said dismally, "but it just won't go up and down."

"What won't?" I gurgled.

"My navel—what else?"

"With all the problems you got to choose from, you have to pick that?" I gaped at her.

"It worries him." She jerked her thumb in the direction of the living room. "A thousand dollars I cost him, he says, and for that kind of money he figures he's entitled to a genuine belly dancer, and if it's genuine it just has to go up and down."

I gave her the right profile as a kind of counterpunch, but it had about the same effect as the left, like nil. This dame was preoccupied I figured, and very probably a nut also.

"Selina, honey," I offered generously. "If you want I'll come around and help you practice?"

"Are you kidding?" she asked coldly. "You've got enough problems of your own already, the way your head keeps twitching from side to side all the time!"

chapter 2

The Ottoman Club was one of the lesser survivors of the belly-dancer boom that hit a couple of years back. It was west of Broadway in the forties, and from outside it looked like a morgue. Inside, it was no improvement; the lights were dim, the drinks dubious, the food suspect. I had gotten there around ten that night and spaced a couple of dubious bourbon on the rocks until the floor show started an hour later. There had been a rapid succession of belly dancers who all looked alike and shimmied alike and left me cold alike. Then they announced Leila Zenta, the exotic dancer.

She was blonde with a deep fringe that hovered a quarter-inch above her eyebrows, while the rest of her hair tumbled down on either side of her face to her shoulders. Her face was more pert than sensual. She looked almost slender in pleasing contrast to the bloated curves of the belly dancers who had gone before. Slender, but even a myopic misanthrope could never have called her flat.

The dance—in a costume of spangled briefs and two glittering stars pasted over the tips of her firm,

NYMPH TO THE SLAUGHTER 17

shapely breasts—was more erotic than exotic, but almost refined by comparison to the endless succession of grinding navels that had gone before. When I heard the thin spattering of applause that greeted the end of her act, I figured I was a minority in the navel field. The blonde inclined her head maybe an inch in acknowledgment, gave the audience a fierce glare of pure hatred, then hurried off. Leila was immediately replaced by another belly dancer—Ishna from Istanbul—and after the first couple of bumps and grinds I figured the Turks had most likely deported her and they had good reason.

I beckoned to the waiter, who came across to my table reluctantly—for him, Ishna was obviously pure Turkish delight.

"You want another bourbon on the rocks?" he croaked.

"I'm a gambling man, pal," I said confidentially. "I bet on anything."

"I ain't a psychiatrist with a couch and all," he said gloomily, "so I just don't got no ambition to hear your life story!"

"I'd bet ten bucks right now," I told him happily, "that if I ask you to get me into Leila Zenta's dressing room without being seen, you'd tell me right off I was out of my mind."

"You're out of your mind!" he snarled.

"So I lost." I gave him the ten bucks and he suddenly lost interest in Ishna's gyrating navel. "You want to bet some more?" I asked him.

"Yeah!" His voice said his mind didn't believe in miracles but what the hell, anyway. "The same thing, maybe?"

"Almost." I smiled encouragingly at him. "Now I bet you fifty bucks if I ask you to get me into Leila Zenta's dressing room without being seen, you'd say sure you could fix it with no trouble at all—for sixty bucks?"

"Yeah!" He breathed heavily through his nose for a few seconds. "What are you, bud, a mind reader?"

"Twenty now"— I handed him two saw bucks— "and the rest when we get there."

"You got yourself a deal!" He nearly grabbed a couple of my fingers along with the money in his eagerness. "The kitchen door is over there." He nodded toward the far side of the room. "You just kind of drift over there and wait while I check on the bouncers, huh?"

I did like he said; everybody was too busy concentrating on Ishna to worry about me, so I finished up with my back to the wall about six feet away from the kitchen door. A couple of minutes crawled past, then the waiter sidled up and gestured for me to follow him. We went through the kitchen—one quick look and I was goddamned glad I hadn't eaten—then into a dingy corridor which swung left, then right, until we finished up outside a door which had "Miss Zenta" chalk-scrawled across it. The waiter tapped gently.

"Who is it?" a feminine voice called sharply.

"Guy out here wants to see you, Miss Zenta," the waiter said nervously.

"What for?"

He looked at me in mute appeal. "You heard the lady—what for?"

"About a friend of hers," I whispered, "guy called Osman Bey."

The waiter nodded gratefully, then repeated what I'd told him out loud. There was a long silence, then she called, "Tell him to wait a minute, will you? I'm changing."

"So you made it, bud!" the waiter whispered happily.

I paid him off and he disappeared so fast I figured maybe now he had enough to make a down payment on Ishna's king-sized charms, which was one hell of a way to waste my money.

Time dragged past while I smoked a cigarette, then the exotic dancer's voice announced I could enter the dressing room. Inside, it was only a big cubicle containing a tall screen across one corner, a closet, and a dresser with a wall mirror over it.

Leila Zenta sat in front of the mirror removing her make-up. I figured she was dressed for the heat because she'd only gotten as far as a white bra and pink panties, then quit right there. She looked a lot more attractive, and a hell of a lot more sexy, than she'd looked under the harsh spotlight out front. Maybe this was shaping up the way a D. Boyd assignment should, I thought hopefully.

"Well?" Her voice had an irritable rasp.

"I'm Danny Boyd," I told her, and gave her the left profile for free.

"That's a good reason to intrude on my privacy— just because you got a name?" she snapped.

"I'm looking for a dame called Marta Murad," I explained patiently. "A good friend of yours, Osman Bey, figures you know where I can find her."

"I never heard of either of them in my whole life before," she grated. "What are you? Some kind of a sex nut? Sneaking into my dressing room, giving me a phony routine about a couple of people I never even heard of before! Just one yelp out of me and the bouncers will come running in here, fold you into a rubber ball, and bounce you right out the front door. You know that?"

"Honey," I said gently, "the time for that routine was while I was still outside in the corridor. The waiter told you it was about a friend of yours—Osman Bey—and if you didn't know from Osman Bey, right then was a real good time to yell for the bouncers. But you didn't, right?"

She swung around slowly on the chair until she faced me directly with a calculating look in her gray eyes.

"I'm telling you I don't know any Osman Bey," she said in a crisp voice. "But you keep telling me I do. Okay—" she shrugged elaborately "—what makes you so sure?"

"Because he told me," I snarled.

"Told you?" Her eyes widened a fraction. "When was this?"

"Late this afternoon, honey," I said. "Right in the middle of all that Turkish bezazz in his Sutton Place penthouse."

"This afternoon?" Her eyes almost popped clean out of their sockets. "That's impossible!"

"Why?" It was my turn to play the straight man.

"Because he—*Ouch!*"

She suddenly leaped out of the chair with a look of exquisite anguish on her face. "That stupid witch of a dresser must have dropped a pin and it's gotten caught up right where I sit!"

She turned her back toward me and leaned forward from the waist, clutching the back of the chair for support.

"Take a look, will you?" she pleaded. "It must be tangled in my pants someplace!"

The thin silk of her panties was stretched taut across the twin curves of her arched rump, proving the guy who wasted his time searching for a needle in a haystack just hadn't lived. I studied the whole area with one penetrating glance, then decided the only efficient way was to start searching one square inch at a time until I'd covered the whole territory. So it would take a little longer—a half hour maybe?—but it would be real efficient.

I hadn't even got started on the first square inch, when a hard gun barrel poked painfully into my left kidney.

"Tell it again," a masculine voice rasped. "That bit about talking to Osman Bey this afternoon in his penthouse!"

The only place the guy could have come from was in back of that screen in the corner of the dressing room, but now it was too late for me to get smart, anyway.

Leila Zenta straightened up, then turned toward me with a derisive grin on her face. "Sucker!" she said contemptuously. "I figured there was one sure way of

NYMPH TO THE SLAUGHTER

stopping you from watching what went on in the mirror."

"Maybe you'd like to introduce me to your friend, Leila?" I asked hopefully. "Tell him that gun in my back makes me real nervous?"

"Sure." She smiled again. "Meet Frankie Lomax—he's the owner."

"Of what, exactly?" I asked.

"The Ottoman Club—" she started.

"And her," the harsh voice from in back of me growled, "and I also own the finger on the trigger, Boyd!" The gun barrel jabbed me painfully, emphasizing the point. "Turn around," he growled, "like real slow, huh?"

I did like the man said, and heard Leila's chair scrape in back of me. The first glimpse of Lomax didn't give me any real confidence. He was a powerfully built guy in his late thirties with a thatch of sandy-colored hair and lifeless eyes set deep under beetling eyebrows. His thin mouth was twisted in a permanent sneer of contempt for the whole goddamned world, and that did include me.

"Why don't you sit down when a lady offers you a chair, Boyd?" he asked conversationally.

A split second later the gun barrel sank brutally into my solar plexus, then slammed into me a second time as my knees buckled, connecting right between my eyes with neat precision. I bounced into the chair Leila had so thoughtfully provided in back of me a few moments before. The whole room spun in a wild kaleidoscope while nausea churned my stomach.

"Relax, Boyd." Lomax's voice sounded faraway and almost gentle. "We're going to have a real heart to heart talk."

Leila moved around beside Lomax and looked down at me with critical disapproval showing in her cold gray eyes.

"I figure he belongs to some rich old dame," she said idly. "One of those Park Avenue bitches who thinks he's more fun to have around the place than a poodle. You think he can bark pretty and balance cookies on his darling damp nose, huh, Frankie?"

"I figure he's going to bark pretty for us right now," he snarled. "Start talking, Boyd!"

"It's like fun-time is over, honey," Leila said sweetly.

My stomach had quietened down to just feeling real nervous, but there was still a sharp throbbing pain right between my eyes. I was in no mood to appreciate their heavy humor—and in no position to voice any disapproval, either.

"I'm looking for a girl called Marta Murad," I said carefully. "Osman Bey told me to talk with Leila Zenta and here I am."

The gun barrel rapped the bridge of my nose hard enough to bring tears to my eyes.

"Don't fool around with me, Boyd," Lomax whispered. "I eat punks like you for breakfast. Corlis sent you, right?"

"Corlis?" I queried painfully. "I don't know any Corlis."

"So play it cute," he said slowly, "and maybe I'll drop you into Oyster Bay and you'll come up right onto the Corlis beach, but by the time you do come up, Boyd, you won't be smelling like roses!"

"Frankie, old buddy—" I said with restraint, "I hope you don't mind me calling you old buddy. We seem to have gotten along together so well in such a short time—old buddy, if I knew what you were talking about I'd join in. Honest!"

For a nasty moment I figured I was about to get that gun barrel across the bridge of my nose again, then Lomax suddenly relaxed.

"Okay," he said. "It doesn't matter, anyway. When you get back there, tell that big fat slob the next one that comes snooping around my place will come back dead!"

"How about this one, Frankie?" Leila asked anxiously. "You going to let him just walk out of here?"

"I'm sending him back as a warning to Corlis." Lo-

NYMPH TO THE SLAUGHTER

max smiled thinly. "He's not going back dead—just bent a little."

"Maybe I can help with the bending?" the blonde suggested gleefully.

"Why not?" he agreed.

There was a sudden sharp knock on the door and Lomax frowned irritably. "Get the hell out, I'm busy!" he yelled.

"It's Julie Kern, Lomax, I want to talk." Even the closed door couldn't muffle the metallic sound of the voice.

The door slammed open and a character who looked like he'd just stepped out of one of those glossy magazine advertisements for masculine sartorial elegance "tailored by—" walked into the room. He was maybe in his late thirties, tall and lean, with a casual air of innate authority. His thick black hair was cut a fraction on the short side, his brown eyes had an alert coldness, and his face would have been handsome, like distinguished yet, if it hadn't been for the puckered white scar that drew the corner of his mouth down into a permanent snarl.

"I'm busy, Julie," Lomax said uncertainly. "Couldn't we make it some other time?"

"Some other time?" the guy said in the same metallic voice that had effortlessly cut through the door a few seconds previously. He made a production out of checking his wafer-thin platinum watch, then smiled slowly. The effect of the permanent snarl on his face was even worse when he smiled, and it was obvious Lomax just didn't care for it at all.

"Some other time?" he repeated again. "When Julie Kern says he wants to talk, then you listen, Frankie. It's that simple."

"Yeah," Lomax said reluctantly. "It's just that—" He waved the gun barrel toward me for a moment. "I'm all tied up right now."

Kern stretched out his right leg, hooked his heel behind the door, and kicked it shut. "I wouldn't want anybody to say I was hard to get along with, Frankie."

His cold eyes slowly stripped Leila naked, bringing a faint flush to her cheeks and a look of sudden fear into her eyes. "So you get yourself untied, and while I'm waiting the broad can keep me amused, huh?"

"No!" Leila said frantically.

"What's the matter, babe?" Kern smiled at her bleakly. "You do tricks, don't you? You're all dressed for it."

"Okay, Julie," Lomax said in a strangled voice. "I guess this will keep. What do you want to talk about?"

"I just got the word from Italy," Kern said flatly. "The Man says it's your problem."

"He—what?" Lomax's face turned ugly. "He can't do this to me, Julie! I never got it—he knows that."

"The Man says he did like you said, and it's your problem," Kern rasped. "You cut it any way you want, the answer's still the same."

"He can't do this to me!" Lomax said thickly. "I won't stand for it, you hear me, Julie! He can't double-cross me like this and get away with it!"

"You got a big mouth, Frankie," Kern said and smiled at him. "You keep leaving it wide open all the time and somebody could be tempted to ram something down it, like the sawn-off barrel of a shotgun, you know?"

"Don't lose your temper, honey," Leila said in a shaky voice. "It doesn't do any good!"

"I'll talk to him!" Lomax almost strangled on the words.

"You'll talk to him?" Kern laughed silently. "Nobody does that, Frankie. The Man talks and you listen! He says he's getting awful tired of waiting, like he's been real patient with you all this time but now he's got a nasty feeling the whole deal smells. So he's giving you another forty-eight hours to produce the merchandise."

"He knows I'm doing my goddamn best to come up with it," Lomax said with a haggard look on his face. "You know it, Julie!"

"The Man says either the merchandise or its value—

NYMPH TO THE SLAUGHTER 25

in cash," Kern went on, like he hadn't heard a word Frankie said. "He's not real worried either way."

"I just don't have that kind of money!" Lomax muttered.

Kern fingered his tie—the discreet diagonal bars of color probably fingered the wearer as an officer of some exclusive English Guards regiment—then lifted his shoulders a fraction.

"The Man says no merchandise, no money, I got to take steps, Frankie." He cocked his thumb and index finger, pointing them at Lomax in a childish imitation of a gun, then flicked his thumb.

"You wouldn't!" Leila said shrilly.

"Are you kidding?" he asked her seriously.

"It's not right," Lomax muttered. "You hear me, Julie?"

Kern lost interest and gazed idly around the room for a moment before he nodded toward me. "What's that?"

"He's nothing," Frankie said sullenly. "A fink who's about to collect a couple of unpleasant memories to take home with him, that's all."

"Don't spoil the suit," Kern said casually. "It's not real bad. First time I ever saw a fink dress in style."

"Maybe that's because you never met a fink with a private detective's license before?" I said.

He froze momentarily, then his full concentration hit me with almost physical impact. "A private eye?"

"Don't pay any attention to this punk," Lomax said sharply. "He's lying in his teeth."

"Shut up," Kern told him conversationally. "A private eye has to have a client, right?"

"A client who figures Lomax not only kidnaped his partner's daughter, but also a fortune in diamonds along with her," I said quickly.

"You keep running off at the mouth, Boyd!" Lomax snarled, and raised his gun ready to slam the barrel down across my face again.

"Hold it!" Kern almost purred. "I want to hear

more of this, Frankie. It's like suddenly I'm intrigued."

The hand holding the gun dropped to his side as Lomax looked at Kern in frustrated fury. For the moment his whole concentration was centered on the immaculately dressed character standing just inside the door, and I figured it was about the best moment I was likely to be offered in the immediate—and what promised to be painful—future.

I came out of the chair real fast, my right hand grabbing the gun barrel and twisting it viciously while the stiffened fingers of my left hand slammed into Lomax's solar plexus. He went backwards a couple of paces, his face suddenly gray as he folded in the middle. I jerked the gun free of his grasp as he went and quickly reversed my grip so now I held it in the approved style, by the butt.

chapter 3

Leila Zenta just stood there wide-eyed, with a look on her face that said she didn't believe it. I wasn't worried about Lelia because I'd seen already she didn't have any concealed weapons about her person —well, not in the conventional sense anyway. It was the well-dressed creep I was more worried about.

"Frankie must be getting soft, his reflexes are shot to hell," Julie Kern said in a nearly amiable voice. "I guess it must be all those belly dancers—they look like an exhausting hobby."

The fingers of his right hand crept inside his coat while he was talking, in a slow, almost imperceptible movement.

"You wouldn't want messy blood all down the front of your expensive suit, would you, Julie?" I asked in a tone of voice that matched his in near amiability.

His hand stopped its creeping movement and dropped down to his side. "You got a suspicious nature, private detective fink," he said easily.

"Boyd is the name," I told him. "Danny Boyd."

"It's forgettable!"

Frankie Lomax straightened up painfully and gave

me a look that promised swift bloody murder at the first opportunity he could grab.

"Why don't you sit down, Frankie?" I gestured with the gun toward the chair I'd only vacated a couple of seconds before. "You look all pooped."

He said a few short words that were expressive if not educational, then I punctuated his syntax with a sharp rap of the gun barrel across the bridge of his nose. It was like *touché,* and learning the right meaning of that word once cost me a backhanded slap across the profile from a French blonde who only lay down because she was tired.

"Well—" Kern shrugged gently. "Whatever the problem is, I guess you boys are about to sort it out between you, so I'll be moving along."

"Don't be in a hurry, Julie," I suggested, then pointed the gun at him for a clincher. "Stick around awhile —there'll be a whole bunch of good clean fun. I may even knock Frankie's teeth right down his throat."

"Don't you dare touch him, you son of a bitch!" Leila said fiercely. "Don't you dare lay another finger on him!"

"Only if I have to, honey," I said honestly. "I figure he's got Marta Murad hidden away someplace and I want to find out where. All you got to do, Frankie, old buddy, is take me there and the whole bit will be painless, I guarantee it."

Lomax made an interesting but entirely impractical suggestion about what I could do as an alternative. I whipped the gun barrel across his throat and it was Leila who cried out in agony. It was interesting and also logical because Frankie's vocal chords were temporarily paralyzed right then. Kern watched with a bored expression on his face, like he was watching the rerun of a movie he's seen a thousand times before.

"Honey"—I grinned bleakly at the blonde— "I'm just a naturally bad-tempered guy. If he won't do like I say, I'll have to get rough. "Her hostile gray eyes spelled out my past, present, and future, if she ever got the chance of reorganizing them. "The trouble with

NYMPH TO THE SLAUGHTER

getting rough," I continued easily, "is that the damage gets to be permanent. Why don't you tell him to be sensible? I mean, who wants a boy friend with a broken nose and no teeth?"

She shuddered slowly and closed her eyes for a moment. "Frankie?" Her voice was flat. "He means it, you don't have any choice."

Lomax gave a strangled grunt, then shook his head violently.

"Well—" I raised the gun in the air slowly.

"Wait!" There was fierce decision in Leila's voice. "You're wrong, Boyd. I'll prove it to you."

"How?"

"I'll show you who he *has* got stashed away in the club," she said stiffly.

"You figure that's a real smart idea, baby?" Julie asked in his metallic voice.

"I'm not about to just stand here and watch him butcher Frankie, even if you are," she snarled. "Is it a deal, Boyd?"

Lomax made some frantic gurgling sounds deep in his throat that didn't make any sense, but I guessed they signified he didn't approve of the idea at all.

"It's a deal, Leila," I told her. "But if it's not on the level—"

"I need a robe," she said.

She went across to the closet, opened the door, took out a black silk robe, and slipped it into it.

"That closet have a key?" I queried.

"Sure." She looked mildly surprised at the stupid question.

"Then leave it open for a moment," I told her. "It's just the place for Frankie—like a recovery room, even."

Lomax stared at me viciously for a long moment, then lurched onto his feet and walked across to the closet. I waited until he'd gotten inside, then looked at Kern.

"Just two things, Julie," I said politely. "You take

out your gun—real slow—and drop it onto the floor. Then you join Frankie in the closet, right?"

"Don't push it, Boyd," he whispered.

"No more than I have to, Julie," I said sincerely.

He hesitated for a moment, then shrugged gracefully. A couple of seconds later his gun dropped onto the floor, and I watched him carefully all the way across to the closet. Once he was inside, I told Leila to close the door and lock it, then bring me the key. She dropped it into my hand a moment later, her face set in a taut mask.

"Do we go now?" she snapped.

"Sure, honey," I told her. "I'm going to stay real close to you all the time—like, no snappy conversation with anybody we meet on the way, huh?"

"You don't have to spell it out!"

We went out of the dressing room and I carefully closed the door in back of me and locked it. Then Leila led the way through a maze of narrow corridors until we finished up outside what looked like a door made out of solid steel. There was some kind of gimmick set in the center of it, and even after I'd taken a close look, I still didn't believe it.

"A combination lock?" I said doubtfully.

"It's the wine cellar," Leila said. "Frankie figured anybody could get a duplicate key made, but if only three people know the combination it's easy to check which one of them was the thief if anything is stolen."

"With the kind of booze Frankie sells in this joint, he could leave the door wide open," I said. "Nobody would take any of it as a gift."

"Sometimes he keeps other things down here beside the booze," she said indifferently.

Her fingers spun the dial, the tumblers clicked rhythmically, then she gave a gentle push and the door swung wide open.

"After you, honey," I told her.

She led the way down a short flight of stairs into the cellar. It was a room, maybe twenty by twenty, illumininated by a dim, fly-specked and naked bulb hanging from the ceiling. Around the walls were ancient steel racks that contained a fair variety of booze; some of the bottles were so thick with cobwebs and dust, they'd maybe been there since their contents were originally distilled in a bathtub during Prohibition.

In the center of the room was a pile of packing cases with junk heaped on top of them in an incredible littered confusion. Leila stopped at the bottom of the stairs and called out, "Hey! You got company."

Nobody answered or appeared to acknowledge her polite greeting. She called a second time with the same result.

"If this is some kind of a gag, honey, you're about to regret it," I grated.

"This is no gag," she said tautly. "He's in here someplace—maybe he's asleep or something."

She walked further into the cellar, skirting the mound of junk in the center, until she reached the cleared space in back of it and stopped suddenly. For a moment she looked like she was frozen solid to the one spot, then she gave a thin, high-pitched scream. I caught up with her in a kind of convulsive leap, just as her whole body started shaking uncontrollably.

"You did it," she whispered. "You kept Frankie out of the way while another of Corlis's hoods came here and—" The whites of her eyes showed alarmingly for a couple of seconds, then she crumpled to the floor at my feet.

That made for two bodies on the floor. I knew Leila had only temporily resigned from the human race, but the other body had made a permanent resignation for sure. I knelt down beside it and took a closer look. The body belonged to a little fat guy who lay sprawled on his back with the hilt of a knife protruding from his chest.

From the look on his swarthy face he had died in abject fear, and I guessed with no resistance. Naked terror showed in the wide-open dark eyes and the contorted facial muscles. I searched through the pockets of his suit gingerly and came up with a big fat zero.

Somebody, his murderer most likely, had cleaned them out so there wasn't even a handkerchief left.

I got back onto my feet as Leila whimpered faintly and opened her eyes. A mixture of hate and fear showed in them as she looked up at me. I bent down to help her back onto her feet and froze about halfway as Lomax's voice suddenly boomed from the door at the head of the stairs.

"You didn't figure a closet was about to keep me out of the way, Boyd?" he shouted in a jeering voice. "I wouldn't take a chance on trying to keep you locked in a closet—I'd rather leave you right where you are down in the cellar!"

"I've got your gun down here with me, old buddy," I called back.

"It's a steel door with a combination lock, punk!" he sneered. "Watch out for the ricochet when you start shooting at it!"

"Sure," I said pleasantly. "I'm in no hurry to get out anyway—not with your girl friend down here for company."

Leila's reaction to that wasn't exactly flattering to the profile. She leaped onto her feet, her eyes wide with sheer terror at the thought.

"Frankie!" she yelped despairingly. "You got to get me out of here!"

"Don't worry, honey," he said in a thick voice. "I've got a couple of the boys with me. We'll be right down!"

"Not if you want your girl friend to say healthy," I snarled.

There was a sudden silence while Lomax digested that thought. I waited maybe half a minute to let it sink in, then spoke again. "I'll give you a couple of minutes to get yourself, and your boys, the hell out of my way," I called. "Then I'm coming up—and Leila's coming with me as far as the front door. If I even see you or one of your hoods on the way out, old buddy, the dame's going to suffer some permanent and painful damage!"

NYMPH TO THE SLAUGHTER 33

"Frankie!" the girl screamed hysterically. "Do like he says—he's a murderer!"

There was another long silence while Lomax thought that one over. Finally he answered in the gentle tones of a frustrated homicidal maniac. "All right!" he bellowed. "But I'll get you for this, Boyd, if it takes me the rest of my life!"

I checked my watch. "You got two minutes to disappear, and take your boys with you, Frankie."

He said something unprintable and after that there was no sound from the top of the stairs. Leila stood mutely watching me, her body still quivering gently, and that look of complete terror in her eyes. Now was not the time to tell her I'd had nothing to do with the murder of the guy who lay dead on the floor. While she had me figured for a murderer, or an active accomplice at least, she was going to be tractable. How tractable, I was about to find out.

"What do you think Frankie's doing right now?" I asked conversationally.

"Just like you told him," she said eagerly. "What else?"

"You think he's a smart guy?"

"Sure, Frankie's real smart, he's got brains okay, he—" she faltered nervously. "Well, no, to be honest, Frankie's so dumb he—"

"Sure," I grunted, "that's how I figured it, too."

"What do you mean?"

"Never mind!" I said harshly. "Take off your clothes."

"What?"

"You heard me." I scowled at her ferociously. "Or you want what he just got?" I gestured with the gun toward the corpse on the floor.

For a moment she was about to argue, but then another quick look at the corpse convinced her any fate would be a distinct improvement on his. She turned away from me quickly, slipped out of the robe, unhooked her bra, and peeled off the pink panties—all in a quick economy of movement like a professional stripper working against a time limit.

When she turned back toward me, I saw she had a flawless body and sincerely wished I had both time and opportunity to appreciate the fact. "Fine," I said, "let's go."

We went up the stairs with Leila going first and me right in back of her, the gun barrel nudging the curve of her spine. When we reached the narrow corridor there was nobody in sight. Then we backtracked through the maze of deserted corridors until we reached Leila's dressing room. I remembered that now it was only a right and left turn to bring us back into the kitchen. Maybe the exotic dancer had a lousy memory because she made a left turn.

"Hold it," I said. "This isn't the way to the kitchen."

She stopped obediently. "I figured you'd want the back entrance?"

"Even if you did change your mind about Frankie being a real smart guy," I said, "he couldn't be that dumb!"

"What do you mean?"

"I mean not to have a couple of his boys waiting outside for me to come out the back door," I said pointedly. "So we'll go through the kitchen."

Leila quivered suddenly. "Through the kitchen?" Her voice jumped an octave. "With me like this?"

"Or bleeding a little," I suggested pleasantly. "The choice is yours, honey."

She hesitated for a moment when we came to the swinging doors that led into the kitchen, but a sharp jab from the gun barrel rapidly overcame her reluctance.

"What I need to get out of this joint is a diversion," I told her as we went through the kitchen, ignoring the open-mouthed stares of the chef and a couple of bus boys. "And you're it, you exotic dancer, you!"

Leila stopped again when we reached the far door and looked back at me piteously. "All those people

NYMPH TO THE SLAUGHTER 35

out there in the club!" she whimpered. "You can't want me to go out there like this!"

"They'll love every moment of it," I said confidently. "All you have to do is run straight out onto the floor and start in with your dance."

"The second floor show's started already," she said frantically. "There'll be another dancer out there, right in the middle of her act."

"So what do you care about competition?" I snarled. "Hear this good! If you don't do exactly like I say, I'll put a bullet in the exact spot where you had trouble with that imaginary pin!"

"I wish I was dead!" she moaned helplessly.

I pushed the door open and we stepped out into the darkened club. Suddenly it was my lucky night because Ishna was back under the spotlight again, and the customers were all held enthralled by her wildly gyrating navel.

"Go!" I said, right into Leila's shell-like ear, then gave her a sharp slap across her naked rump for emphasis.

Five seconds later Ishna came to a sudden stop right in the middle of a real free-swinging grind, and it almost left her navel permanently unhinged. Then she watched with a stupefied expression on her face while a stark-naked blonde capered into the spotlight and, without a moment's hesitation, plunged into an exotic dance routine.

The stunned silence from the audience didn't seem to last any time at all; it was immediately followed by a thunderous swell of applause that threatened to tear the chandeliers loose from the ceiling. After that came a confused bedlam of sound as around 90 per cent of the audience knocked over tables and chairs in their mad rush toward the raised dais where Leila danced, to get themselves a completely uninhibited view of the latest entertainment phenomenon in Manhattan.

A couple of bouncers appeared from the foyer and resolutely charged into the back of the milling crowd, completely disappearing from sight a few moments later. I had no trouble at all in walking out of the club at a reasonably leisurely pace.

On the sidewalk the doorman caught my nod and blew his whistle vigorously. A cab stopped a few seconds later and the doorman politely held the rear door open for me. Even out on the street you could hear the frantic cheering and shouting from inside the club.

"Sounds like one of the girls is going over real big tonight," the doorman said interestedly.

"Leila Zenta's doing a passionate cha-cha with Frankie Lomax," I told him as I slid into the back seat of the cab. "Both of them are stark naked."

"You're kidding," he said feebly.

"Maybe you'd better give him this?" I suggested, and dropped Frankie's gun into the palm of his hopefully outstretched hand. "I figure Lomax is almost sure to want to kill himself when it's all over!"

Then I slammed the door shut, the cab pulled away from the curb, and I leaned back against the upholstery and wondered happily just how many encores Leila would give the enraptured audience before she felt sure I had left the place.

chapter 4

It was around eleven the next morning when Fran Jordan stepped into my office with a kind of smug look on her face that meant she knew something I didn't.

Fran is my secretary—a remarkably efficient green-eyed redhead with the kind of figure that should be displayed naked on top of a high mountain so the rest of her sex throughout the world can understand what they're aiming for. She always wears clothes around the office, I admit, for some conventional type of reasoning I've never understood. This morning she looked immaculately cool in a gunmetal orlon blouse and black skirt.

"You remember that impossible thing you asked me to do an hour back?" she said triumphantly. "Well, I've done it!"

"The hell you have?" I looked at her with sudden enthusiasm. "How about giving me a practical demonstration? I always figured it was impossible, even for a professional contortionist!"

She stared at me bleakly for a moment. "My uncle Joe always gets depressed because he works in a sewer. I told him just the other night he doesn't know when he's got it made. 'How would you like working for a sewer—a sewer that talks back?' I asked him, and that shut him up real fast."

"Please don't talk dirty in office hours, Miss Jordan," I said briskly. "A client may walk in at any moment."

"Me talk dirty?" she gasped. "It's you—"

"I talk sexy," I said in a dignified voice. "There's a world of difference."

She swallowed hard a couple of times, while her facial expressions ran a gamut from fury to hopeless resignation. "Ah," she said finally, "what's the use?"

"It's the profile that does it every time," I reminded her in a gentle, chiding voice. "It's irresistible."

Fran sank into a chair with an audible sigh of relief. "I always get dizzy looking at heights," she explained calmly, "and your ego makes the Empire State building look like a brownstone."

I know when I'm licked. "So what was the impossible you just accomplished in the last hour?" I asked quickly.

"Corlis who lives in Oyster Bay?" she said. "There are three of them. One is a widow, one is a retired gentleman who worked for the town engineer's office for forty years, and the last one is a dealer in art, antiques, and all that jazz."

"Rare books, maybe?" I asked hopefully.

"I guess so," she said, nodding.

"He sounds like the guy I'm looking for," I told her. "Where do I find him?"

"He has a gallery on Second Avenue in the forties," Fran said. "His full name is Matthew Corlis."

"You did a great job, honey," I said sincerely. "Maybe I should take you to dinner tonight?"

"Just keep on rewarding my good work that way and I'll resign by the end of the week," she snapped.

"Well, it was worth a try," I admitted. "I think I'll go take a look at Matthew Corlis and his fine arts gallery."

"Don't hurry back," she said, smiling wistfully. "The

office is so pleasant when you're not around. I mean, a girl can adjust her garters without risking a sudden attack on her virtue and all."

"I never catch you adjusting your garters while I'm in the office." I brooded for a moment. "Maybe I should wear sneakers in working hours?"

"That's just the kind of reaction you would have!" Fran got onto her feet quickly. "Is there anything else you want done while you're out?"

"No," I said, then thought again. "Yes! If my new client calls, tell him I'll call him back."

"What's his name?"

"Osman Bey."

There was a derisive glint in her green eyes. "Oh, sure," she said lightly, "and just what is Osman Bey's vocation in life? An agent for a troupe of belly dancers, I wouldn't be surprised!"

"How did you know about the belly dancers?" I asked her.

"Okay," she snorted. "If you want to play secrets with your confidential secretary it doesn't worry me one bit!" Then she flounced out of my office with all the fury of a woman scorned.

For a little while I seriously contemplated telling Fran the whole story about Osman Bey, his slave girl and hookah and all—my visit to the Ottoman Club the previous night and how I'd found a corpse there—how an exotic dancer dancing naked under a spotlight created enough confusion for me to get out of the club in one piece and—it was about there I gave up the whole idea. Who the hell would believe it? In the cold light of morning I had enough trouble believing it myself.

I walked out and Fran's back was turned toward me with ramrod determination as I passed her in the outer office. The only farewell I got was a cold, expressive sniff as I closed the door in back of me. It was different in the old days, I figured, when a guy rode out to do battle, his ever-loving woman kissed him a fervent farewell and gave him her handkerchief or something in ever-loving memory. Of course I also had to remember that once he was out of sight, his ever-loving woman took off hastily in search of the nearest guy with an efficient can opener. In the world of high fashion where every kind of style invariably repeats itself, it's an intriguing puzzle why some nut of a French designer hasn't brought back the chastity belt.

It was around high noon when I stepped off the burning sidewalk of Second Avenue into the cool gloom of Matthew Corlis's fine arts gallery. The inside was no more impressive than the outside—which consisted of one drab display window full of hideous Eastern and Oriental refuse—and the gloom was so thick I was practically blinded once I got inside the door.

"Can I help you?" a purely feline voice purred from out of the darkness.

My eyes finally readjusted and I could see again. Standing squarely in front of me was a girl. Her straight blonde hair was made into a conical-shaped hairdo, swept behind her ears and around the nape of her neck, so it dramatically emphasized the high cheekbones and delicate bone structure of her elfin face. A sharp intelligence gleamed from her cobalt-blue eyes and it made a kind of balance to the provocative curve of her slightly protruding lower lip. The white cotton sweater fit snugly to reveal the forward thrust of her small pointed breasts, while her tight skirt clung to neatly rounded hips and outlined her long shapely legs every time she moved.

"I'm what they call a girl," she said in a faintly amused tone of voice. "I presume you've never seen one before?"

"When I saw all that junk in the window I figured the owner was lying in his teeth by calling it a fine arts gallery," I told her huskily. "Now I've seen you I take it all back."

"I'm sure Mr. Corlis will be enchanted," she said in a mock-demure manner.

I gave her both sides of the profile real slow, because I figured she deserved them. "My name's Danny

NYMPH TO THE SLAUGHTER

Boyd." I smiled encouragingly. "You want me to spell it out while you write it down?"

"I don't think so," she said easily. "It's not a hard name to memorize, Mr. Boyd."

"How about yours?" I queried.

"I'm Kitty Torrence," she said briskly. "Now, what can I do for you, Mr. Boyd?"

"What a wonderful world of fantasy you just opened up for me with that question!" I said fervently.

She closed her eyes for a long moment, took a deep breath, then slowly exhaled and opened her eyes again. "You're still here, of course?" She caught her lower lip between gleaming white teeth and teased it gently. "Well, I've had difficult clients before, but never quite like you, Mr. Boyd. You are a client, I presume?"

"Not exactly," I said. "I wanted to see Mr. Corlis, only it somehow doesn't seem important any more. Why don't you take a little time out to persuade me into becoming a client, Miss Torrence? It could be fun."

"And to think it was last weekend my darling mother asked me what kind of people did I expect to meet, working in a Second Avenue junk shop!" the blonde murmured. "You offer a tempting proposition, Mr. Boyd, although I already have the feeling I could regret it. But I would like to sell *something* before I quit."

"We could start with lunch," I suggested eagerly.

"That sounds reasonably safe—only I'm not sure I'd trust that profile in a cross-town bus even!—all right, Mr. Boyd, you just made yourself a deal."

"Great!" I said. "Let's go."

"I'm not on my lunch hour yet," she murmured. "My hour of midday freedom starts at one. That gives you plenty of time to see Mr. Corlis, don't you think?"

"I'm crazy about girls with brains," I told her with open admiration. "Especially the ones who are also blonde and beautiful, too."

"Mr. Corlis has an office right at the far end of the gallery," she said slowly. "He's there right now. Or I think he is—somehow, I'm just not sure of anything any more."

"It's the humidity," I assured her. "An air-conditioned lunch will work miracles."

"Please go see Mr. Corlis now?" She closed her eyes tight again. "I have enough confusion for the time being, Mr. Boyd."

I reluctantly walked past her, then down the length of the gallery, the *objets d'art* on either side of me becoming progressively uglier with each step I took, until I came to a frosted glass door. I knocked sharply on it.

"Come in, if you please," a gentle voice answered.

The office was just big enough to hold a couple of dusty steel cabinets, an ancient roll-top desk, and the guy sitting in back of it.

"Corlis?" I said curtly.

"I am Matthew Corlis." He stood up behind the desk as if to prove the point.

Corlis was a thin little guy who stood a couple of inches over five feet tall at most. Baldness accentuated his high-domed forehead to a point where it looked almost grotesque, and his face, like his personality, seemed completely colorless. The washed-out blue eyes were never still—always moving in their sockets like they were looking for some means of escape.

I stared at him blankly, trying to reconcile the factual reality of the man with Frankie Lomax's description of him the previous evening as a "big fat slob." Maybe it had been Frankie's idea of a joke, only I still couldn't believe he had a sense of humor buried under all that nervous viciousness.

"What can I do for you, sir?" Corlis asked in a soft voice.

What he could do for me was give me some information about any one of a dozen things I didn't understand right then. I figured I might as well try them on him for size, one at a time.

"The Man sent me," I snarled.

He blinked a couple of times. "Ah—which man was that, sir?"

NYMPH TO THE SLAUGHTER 43

So I'd struck out on the first try. "My name's Boyd," I said roughly. "Danny Boyd. Maybe you heard of me after what happened in the Ottoman Club last night?"

"I'm afraid not, Mr. Boyd." It sounded like geniune regret in his voice. "Ottoman Club, you said? What an unusual name! An ottoman is a type of couch, you know?"

"Never mind!" I gurgled. "Maybe you never heard of Julie Kern either?"

A look of vague interest showed in his faded eyes for a moment. "Is she a dealer, too?" He didn't even get the sex right.

"Okay," I said heavily. "Why don't we stop being cute, Mr. Corlis? You want to tell me you never heard of Frankie Lomax?—or Marta Murad?—maybe you never even heard of Osman Bey?"

Corlis sat down again suddenly and fumbled with some papers on the desk in front of him for a few moments.

"Just precisely what is the—ah—purpose of your visit here, Mr. Boyd?" he asked in a nervous voice.

"A girl called Marta Murad was kidnaped five days back," I said in a threatening voice. "A man called Osman Bey hired me to find her, so I went looking for her in the Ottoman Club last night. But the owner—Frankie Lomax—wouldn't believe I'd come from Osman Bey because he was so goddamned sure you'd sent me! I want to know why, friend? I'm prepared to stay right here until you tell me!"

He shuffled the papers on his desk some more, then looked up at me with obvious reluctance. "I find this difficult to explain, Mr. Boyd," he whispered. "Let me say this—I understand your problem but you've made a basic mistake in your whole premise."

"What kind of double talk is that?" I grated.

"Please, Mr. Boyd!" He held up his hand in a defensive gesture. "If you would be kind enough to step outside the office for a moment while I make a phone call, I may be able to render you some assistance."

"All right," I said reluctantly. "But make it fast, huh?"

"It won't take long, I promise you."

I went out of the office and the glass-paneled door closed in back of me so fast it nearly caught my foot. The view of Kitty Torrence standing at the front of the gallery with her back toward me was interesting enough to keep me occupied for the next five minutes. Then the door opened again, and Corlis's bald head peeped around the frame. "Won't you come back in, Mr. Boyd?" he asked shyly.

By the time I got back inside, he was already established in his chair again. For a little time he just looked at me with a vague spark of interest in his eyes, then he planted both elbows firmly on the desk and neatly steepled his fingertips together.

"Let me explain my—ah—situation, sir, if you please?" His voice trembled nervously. "I am a dealer in the finer things of life and here in my gallery this is the only kind of business ever transacted. However —ah—compelling your curiosity is, Mr. Boyd, I am sure it can be satisfied by a meeting later at my home on Long Island. Are you agreeable to that?"

"Maybe," I grunted. "When?"

"This evening, perhaps. Shall we say six o'clock?"

"How do I get there?"

He gave me precise, detailed instructions on how to reach Oyster Bay, and the exact location of his house once I arrived in the area.

"You wouldn't be stalling me, Mr. Corlis?" I said coldly.

"I assure you, sir, that is my last intention."

"For your sake, Mr. Corlis, I hope you're right," I told him, "or the chances are it will be your last intention!"

"Until this evening then, Mr. Boyd?" His voice trembled worse than before. "Good day, sir."

"Until this evening, Mr. Corlis," I said courteously, then put both hands on the edge of his desk and leaned toward him ominously. "I sincerely hope you're not stalling me, friend—" I give him an ugly smile "—because frankly, you're just not built for it. My guess is if I grabbed you with both hands and pulled at the same time, you'd snap clean in half!"

When I walked out of his office he was still frantically trying to burrow through the back of his chair.

Kitty Torrence took a long, lingering look around the second most expensive restaurant in Manhattan, and sighed happily.

"This is my idea of living," she confided. "It makes such a lovely contrast with the corner drugstore I lunch at every day!"

"I'd figure you were lucky Corlis can afford to pay you any salary at all," I said. "Does he ever sell any of that junk?"

"Put it this way, Mr. Boyd—"

"Danny!" I corrected her.

"—Danny. In the month I've been working at the gallery I've never sold anything." She raised her third martini and lowered the level in the glass at least an inch before she took it away from her lips again. "You can call me Kitty," she said thoughtfully. "You know why?"

"Tell me?" I suggested brilliantly.

"Because I know exactly what you've got in mind and I don't really disapprove, I mean, what's life but experience, anyway? So if you were still calling me 'Miss Torrence,' when we got around to making love it would just break me up." She raised her glass again, then looked at me seriously over the rim for a moment.

"Laughter is the death knell of sex!" she announced in a grave voice.

I looked at her admiringly. "How come you know all the answers already—and you're so young?"

"I started asking the questions at a very early age," she said smugly. "About the time you decided a crew cut could make you look a little younger, Danny."

It was time for an abrupt change of subject, I

figured. "How does Corlis stay in business if he never sells anything?" I queried.

"I didn't say that," she said in a reproving voice. "I said I hadn't sold anything. Maybe Mr. Corlis has a million mail-order clients who never even come near the place. He must have *some* clients, he keeps on buying more junk all the time."

"Where does he buy it from?"

"All over," she said, shrugging easily. "You should see his file drawers—to say nothing of that desk he stuffs things into! Invoices and accounts everywhere, and everything in a mess, but he always can find things somehow."

"He must buy all over the world, huh?" I queried.

"Sure," she said. "Europe, the Middle East, the Orient. It's a geography lesson in itself to just look at those account names."

A waiter removed her empty glass and replaced it with her fourth martini while she watched with happy approval.

"I have a friend in the same line of businesss," I mentioned in a casual voice. "Guy called Osman Bey."

"Osman Bey?" Kitty had that cliché look on her face for a moment that says the world sure is a small place, yessir. "Mr. Corlis buys from him! I've seen the names of some of the accounts."

"What a coincidence!" I said in amazement. "How about that?"

A sudden shrewd look showed in her cobalt eyes. "Are you putting me on, Danny?"

"Why would I want to do that?" I asked innocently.

"I don't know." She nibbled her lower lip for a moment. "But I have a feeling—"

"I guess we should eat," I said. "That's your fourth martini, you know that?"

"What are you, Danny Boyd, some kind of party pooper?" she asked frostily. "You think I can't hold my liquor, or something?"

She drank the whole martini in one long gulp, then

NYMPH TO THE SLAUGHTER

stared at me intently while her eyes swam in and out of focus.

"Something bothering you, Kitty?" I asked nervously.

"You could have told me," she said in a brooding voice. "Now I feel embarrassed, in a fancy restaurant like this and all."

"Told you what?"

"Look, Danny." Her glassy eyes tried hard to be kind. "I don't really mind you having two heads, but please don't ever let them talk to one another, huh?"

chapter 5

I got back to the office around three. Food, and no more martinis, had made Kitty Torrence practically sober again by the time I returned her to the fine arts gallery. We had a firm date for tomorrow night, I would pick her up at her apartment around eight, and the world was definitely a brighter place.

Fran Jordan looked at me like I was something that should have stayed out of sight as I walked past her into my office. She came in a minute later with the same expression still on her face.

"No word from the belly dancer's agent," she said acidly.

"Oh?" I said, real quick.

"Admit it," she sniffed. "He's just one of your corny gags, huh?"

"He's real—honest!" I assured her. "See, his partner's daughter was kidnaped and Osman daren't tell Abdul Murad—"

"Abdul who?"

"Murad."

"Oh, brother!" Fran looked at me with a sardonic gleam in her eyes. "What's his daughter called?—Fatima?" She stalked out of my office with derisive disbelief showing in every gentle wiggle of her proudly curved rear end.

I lit a cigarette and wondered what had gotten into everybody lately. Why they were all convinced I was putting them on every time I opened my mouth. The sober truth, I figured sourly, was that everybody was putting *me* on, most likely. Only they were doing it for real, not for fun. If it hadn't been for the prospect of the following night spent in the enchanting company of Kitty Torrence, the world would have seemed a dismal place.

Five minutes later Fran was back in the office with a shaken look on her face. "Danny?" she said, smiling nervously. "There's somebody outside wants to see you right away."

"So they're anonymous?" I grunted.

Her smile grew even more nervous. "It's a man."

"Like Mr. X, the head of the big international spy syndicate?" I snarled.

She looked away and shuffled her feet for a moment. "He says his name's Abdul Murad," she admitted in a muffled voice. "I—I guess I was all wrong and you weren't kidding me along, huh?"

"You sure he's not just a figment of my imagination?" I asked icily. "Maybe if you just snap your fingers he'll disappear?"

"So I apologize," she moaned. "Do you want to see him?"

"Sure, send him right in."

The man who strode determinedly into my office a few seconds later was of medium height, but the erect military bearing made him seem taller. He was about fifty, I guessed, with a bristling gray crew cut and a lean sardonic face. The dark eyes sparkled in his swarthy face with an intelligent ferocity and single-minded purpose—the type of guy who can make a good friend or a very bad enemy. From the way he looked at me I figured I had no chance of becoming his friend.

"Mr. Boyd?" His voice was crisp with almost no trace of a foreign accent at all. "I am Abdul Murad."

"Mr. Murad," I said politely. "Won't you sit down?"

"I have no time for formalities or the polite niceties that go with them," he snapped. "I need information from you, and I need it quickly!"

"Information?" I queried. "What about?"

"My daughter was kidnaped five days back," he said tightly. "I have just left the whining dog who was once my partner—Osman Bey. He told me he had not dared go to the police for fear of endangering my daughter's life, but he had hired you—a private detective—to find her!"

"So?" I said.

"I want to know what progress you have made, Boyd. I want an exact detailed account of what you've achieved so far—where you've been, the people you've met, the theories you've formed—I want to know everything!"

"Mr. Murad," I said carefully. "Believe me, I sympathize with the way you must feel right now, having just discovered your daughter's been kidnaped and all. But I can't do it."

"What?" His eyes blazed wildly. "What do you mean —you can't?"

"I can't give you a report of any progress I've made, or anything else concerning the case for one good reason," I told him, "Osman Bey is my client—not you."

"She is *my* daughter!" he snarled. "That gives me a greater right than Osman Bey."

"Not by me," I said truthfully. "I'm sorry, Mr. Murad, but that's how it is."

He came closer to my desk and I could almost feel the frustration and fury boiling inside him. "You'll tell me what I have to know, Boyd," he said in a low-pitched voice, "or I'll beat it out of you!"

I slid open the top drawer of my desk and took out the .357 Magnum. "Cool off, Mr. Murad," I growled. "When my client tells me to talk to you, I'll talk. But not before."

NYMPH TO THE SLAUGHTER   51

He looked at the gun in my hand and for a moment it wasn't about to stop him, then sanity prevailed. "All right, Boyd," he said thickly. "For the moment I can do nothing. But the time will soon come—because I shall make sure it does—when the situation is reversed. Then you will deeply regret that once you refused to help me!"

"How did you just happen to be in New York and discover your daughter was missing?" I asked him.

"I called her long distance from Paris yesterday morning," he said in a bleak monotone. "I thought to pleasantly surprise her. The hotel told me she had checked out only two hours after arrival, without leaving any forwarding address. At first I was stunned by the news, then thought there was probably a reasonable explanation so I called my partner."

A nervous tick throbbed violently in his cheek for a few seconds. "Osman Bey was very nervous and evasive when I spoke with him. She had merely changed hotels, he said, because she didn't care for the first one. When I asked him for the name of her new hotel, he became almost hysterical, spluttering nonsense about how he would gladly die to protect my daughter. He swore on the Koran to see her safely returned to me. I caught the next available plane from Paris and arrived in New York this morning. I came straight to your office after a four-hour session with my former partner."

His lower lip curled contemptuously. "Even his best friend would not say Osman is a brave man! But for once in his miserable life something is more frightening to him than I. He swears he knows no reason why my daughter should have been kidnaped. On his own admission there has been no contact with her kidnapers—no ransom note—nothing! Yet he is sure that to go to the police would endanger her life. Does that make any sense to you, Boyd?"

"Sure, it does," I told him. "Kidnaping is a capital crime in this country. So if the kidnapers think that killing their victim may lessen their chances of being caught, they have nothing to lose because they already face the death penalty."

Murad looked at me steadily for maybe ten seconds. "I ask you again, Boyd. Tell me what progress you have made toward finding my daughter."

"I'll tell you again," I said evenly. "When Osman Bey says it's okay to do that, I'll do it."

"Very well," he said stiffly. "I can't argue with that gun in your hand at the moment."

He turned and walked toward the door with a ramrod back, then stopped when he reached it and glanced over his shoulder at me. "You will regret this, Boyd," he said softly, with no melodramatics in his voice at all. "I make a bad enemy." A moment later the door closed behind him.

I hardly had time to think about it before Fran bounced into the office again.

"Don't tell me Murad's waiting outside for a second round?" I growled.

She shook her head dismally. "My cup runneth over," she confessed. "There's a female on the line says she's calling for Mr. Osman Bey."

I lifted my phone and said, "Boyd."

"This is Selina," a listless voice said in my ear.

The sudden vision of a slave girl whose wonderfully endowed curves were inadequately contained by a red silk vest and baggy silk pants popped unheralded in front of my eyes.

"How are all your little problems, Selina?" I asked her. "Have you got it going up and down yet?"

"Never mind that, fink," she said icily. "I got a message for you from Mr. Bey. He says he had to go out for a while in a hurry and he don't know when he'll be back. But he says to tell you Abdul Murad's in town and whatever you do, you don't tell him anything, understand?"

"Sure," I consoled her. "He's been and gone already and I told him nothing."

"Yeah." She didn't sound enthusiastic. "Anyway, that's about all, I guess. Oh, there was one other thing.

NYMPH TO THE SLAUGHTER 53

Mr. Bey says to tell you he'll call about nine to get your report."

"You tell him I don't know where I'll be around nine tonight," I said truthfully. "So I'll call him first chance I get."

"He won't like that."

"Now you got me crying, honey," I said in a reproachful voice. A moment later there was a sharp click as she hung up.

I put down the phone and saw Fran was looking at me with an undisguised gleam of curiosity in her eyes. "What's she got that should go up and down, Danny?"

"Her navel, what else?" I said without thinking.

"Huh?"

"The art of belly dancing depends on a vertical movement of the navel, they tell me," I explained. "She's worried because Osman Bey figures she cost him a thousand bucks and for that kind of money he's entitled to a genuine vertical movement."

Fran gave a ghastly imitation of a smile. "Well, I didn't believe in Osman Bey, or Abdul Murad, and look where that got me! Okay, I'll take your word for it and I'm not about to ask how he came to pay a thousand dollars for her in the first place, because you'll tell me it's a seller's market in belly dancers right now, right?"

"Well, kind of," I agreed.

"That is"—she bared her teeth painfully once more—"in the slave market on Times Square where he bought her, right?"

"Sure," I agreed in a nonchalant voice. "On the other hand there's a buyer's market in eunuchs, if you're looking for a houseman to keep your apartment real neat."

She made a faint moaning sound and tottered out of my office on dragging feet. Even her back view had a limp look and that was something I would have figured was an impossibility for any dame built the way Fran Jordan was built. I suddenly remembered my date with Corlis out at his Long Island home at six that evening, and took the shoulder harness out of the drawer where it had kept the .357 Magnum company. Maybe I was about to make like Daniel by visiting Corlis in his own den, and I'd feel a hell of a lot happier about the whole deal with a gun along.

From where I was parked on the crest of a hill, the view was almost perfect. A cool, salt-laden breeze took the edge off the heat of the late afternoon sun. Far out on the Sound a yacht spread its white sails against a pink and gold sky, lightly daubed with a few innocuous patches of cloud.

I lifted my binoculars again and took another look at the Corlis house—a solid English-manor type building, perched close to the edge of a cliff which dropped sheer to the beach a couple of hundred feet below. An eight-foot brick wall surrounded the property, surmounted by two strands of electrified wire, so it needed a professional pole vaulter to clear the top of the fence.

My glasses picked out the kennels some fifty feet in back of the house and I wondered what breed of dog Corlis kept there—it figured they'd be wild wolfhounds imported from Siberia. It wasn't a house in the usual sense of the word—it was a fortress. Nobody, short of a small combat group, would have a hope in hell of breaking into the place.

I checked my watch and saw it was five of six, then I drove slowly down the hill and parked in front of the massive gates fashioned from two-inch steel bars. Set in one of the massive stone gateposts was a neat telephone box. I lifted the phone from the hook and pressed the button beside it a couple of times. Maybe ten seconds later a man's voice said, "House."

"My name's Boyd," I told him. "I have an appointment with Mr. Corlis at six."

"Hold it," the voice snapped. I waited patiently another ten seconds before he spoke again. "Okay, you're expected. The gates operate on remote control, so when they open you drive right in and up to the house—got it?"

NYMPH TO THE SLAUGHTER

"Sure," I told him, and he hung up.

By the time I got back to the car the gates were already opening slowly. When the space was big enough I drove through onto the driveway, and stopped in the flagged parking area out front of the house a short time later. As I walked up onto the front porch, the door opened suddenly and a woman smiled a polite greeting.

Buxom was the polite word for the way she was built, and *fat* the more objective one. She wore a chintzy, floral-patterned dress with a high-standing collar. There was a soft blue tint through the natural gray of her hair which suited her; the elegant hair-do must have taken a full morning at the beauty parlor. Her plump cheeks were youthfully firm and her mouth determinedly cheerful. The only doubtful item in the catalogue of a suburban matron's assets, was her eyes. Their vivid blue color had the quality of a hard lacquer that was guaranteed never to soften or crack.

"Mr. Boyd," she said brightly. "I am Beatrice Corlis. How do you do."

"Hello, Mrs. Corlis," I said politely.

"Won't you come in?"

She led the way through the wide front hall into a massive living room with an ultramodern bar set up at the far end. After she had settled herself comfortably in an armchair, she gestured for me to take a chair opposite her.

"Matthew was delayed leaving his gallery," she said, "but I expect him at any moment now, Mr. Boyd."

The lacquer-brilliant eyes made a detailed survey starting at the crew cut and working their way down unhurriedly. By the time she'd finished I felt like a pound of hamburger steak on the scale, naked and exposed to the mercy of the consumer's cold-blooded judgment.

"I do so hate this hot weather, don't you, Mr. Boyd?" A synthetic smile curved her lips. "And it's so much worse for all you poor businesmen cooped up in that oven of a city! It doesn't give you any chance to fight the heat, does it, having to wear those horrid suits and all." Her eyelids fluttered coquettishly. "We girls are lucky—a nice light dress and hardly anything at all on underneath!"

"Sure," I muttered glassily.

"You must forgive me, Mr. Boyd!" The laugh was strictly girlish by intent. "I just ramble on and on sometimes. Are you one of my husband's business associates? I mean, are you interested in the fine arts, rare *objets d'art,* and suchlike?"

"I have a special interest in your husband's whole field of activity right now, Mrs. Corlis," I said carefully. "So I'm interested in everything he handles at the moment—except antiques."

A savage gleam flared momentarily in back of her eyes to show that antique crack had gotten home. Then the full veneer was back firmly in place.

"I'm sure you'd like a drink, Mr. Boyd."

"It sounds like a wonderful idea," I told her.

"Just press that buzzer over there, under the bar top, will you?" She nodded approval. "That's right! Men are always so clever around the house, aren't they? It didn't take you a second to locate—" An expensive purring sound grew steadily louder as another car came up the drive. "Ah! That will be Matthew now. I'm so glad he's not late. Manhattan must be simply an inferno on a day like this! Now he can cool off and enjoy an evening at home."

A guy dressed in a white waiter's coat and black pants came into the room. He was young, twenty-three at most, and his thick black hair was glossy with that greasy kid stuff they talk about on TV. It matched the glossy look of conceit on his face.

"You rang—madame?" His voice had a deliberate touch of insolence.

"Yes, Michael." She turned toward him, one hand unconsciously primping the already immaculate hairdo. "We'd like a drink. A Scotch Old Fashioned for me I think. How about you, Mr. Boyd?"

"A martini would be fine," I said.

"Better make that two martinis, Michael," she simpered. "I just heard Mr. Corlis come up the driveway."

The kid slouched out of the room like he was doing everybody a big favor by making the drinks. A few seconds after he'd left, Matthew Corlis came into the room with a kind of crablike shuffle. He looked at his wife and his eyes immediately shifted their gaze, saw me, and rolled wildly toward the ceiling.

"Nice to see you again, Mr. Corlis," I said gently.

"I—ah—yes, indeed, Mr. Boyd." He grimaced nervously. "It's hot, don't you think?"

"Maybe that's because of the heat wave, dear?" His wife gave him a murderous look. "Really, Matthew! Do sit down and be still for a moment! You make me feel positively fatigued the way you keep jumping up and down all the time!"

Corlis collapsed onto the couch with a martyred expression, then shuffled his feet in mute outrage. Michael, the kid dressed like a waiter, came back with the drinks and served them with a condescending air.

"I thought you might like your pre-dinner martini now, dear," Mrs. Corlis said.

Corlis lowered his glass, already half empty, from his lips and smiled vaguely. "That was most—ah—kind of you, dear."

The next quarter-hour drifted past with Beatrice Corlis making all the conversational gambits, and taking most of them right back for herself before anyone else got the chance. It didn't bother me too much, I was more interested in watching her husband. The little guy was nothing but an underweight frame strung together by nervous tension. After the first couple of minutes, he sat on the edge of the couch nursing his empty glass with a look of sheer misery on his face. That "pre-dinner martini" jazz had spelled it out—his wife wanted him to have the one drink only, and he didn't have the nerve to question it. I just didn't get it.

Finally Beatrice Corlis ran out of conversation and sat for a whole thirty seconds without saying a word. The silence made Matthew wriggle even worse.

"You know, Mr. Boyd," he suddenly burst out in obvious desperation, "I've found the—ah—perfect answer to the heat!"

"What's that?" I asked politely.

"Air conditioning," he said simply, and closed his eyes tight.

"Why don't you run along now, dear?" his wife said in a tone of casual command. "I'd like to have a little chat with Mr. Boyd on my own for a while."

"Of course." He leaped onto his feet and bounced a couple of times like a remote control pogo stick. "A pleasure, Mr. Boyd." He bowed toward me with grave courtesy. "I much enjoyed our conversation."

"But—" It was too late, he was out of the room already.

"Well," Beatrice Corlis said briskly, "I think we need another drink. I don't like to embarrass Matthew by drinking in front of him when he's limited to just one drink a day. He has to watch his ulcer, you know?"

"It sounds like a macabre pastime," I snarled.

"Ye—es," she said doubtfully. "Would you mind pressing the buzzer again, Mr. Boyd. Two rings this time?"

I did as she said, then sat down again heavily, wondering what the hell Corlis was trying to pull by leaving me saddled with his wife's dull conversation.

Her fingers suddenly drummed a restless tattoo on the arm of her chair for a few seconds, while she glared at me with dispassionate contempt.

"Was it necessary to frighten poor little Matthew half to death with that big act at lunch-time in his gallery, Boyd?" she asked crisply. "I mean, what was it meant to prove?"

I gaped at her open-mouthed without finding a coherent answer to her question.

"You must have known he'd call me right away," she sneered. "Why not come to me in the first place?"

The previous night Frankie Lomax had presumed it was Corlis who'd sent me to his club. It hadn't even occurred to me that "Corlis" could be a woman. "That big fat slob," Frankie said, and I'd wondered if he'd been joking when I met Matthew Corlis with his big head and tiny shrunken frame—but it was a description that fit Beatrice Corlis like a glove.

The kid dressed like a waiter came back into the room with a gun in his hand and in back of him was a second guy, who also had a gun in his hand.

chapter 6

"Michael you know," Mrs. Corlis said pleasantly. "But you haven't met Tino yet." She waved her hand toward the guy in back of the kid. "This is Mr. Boyd, Tino."

Tino was a sallow-faced character with thinning black hair brushed straight back from his forehead; he wore needle-pointed patent leather shoes to match the rich Italian silk suit that fit him like skin. When you looked straight into his eyes all you got was a perfectly mirrored reflection of your own face. It was that peculiarly dead look of the hood turned professional killer, and it didn't reassure me one little bit.

"Tino," I said politely.

He shrugged his thin shoulders irritably, then looked at Mrs. Corlis. "Conversation, you need?" he asked coldly.

"You're right, Tino," she said good-humoredly. "What we need is a little organization. Michael, make us a fresh drink while Tino relieves Mr. Boyd of that lethal whatever-it-is he's got tucked away so snugly in a shoulder harness!"

The kid moved in back of the bar to prepare the

NYMPH TO THE SLAUGHTER 61

drinks, while Tino, the gun in one hand pressed against my forehead, lifted the Magnum from under my left armpit and tossed it carelessly onto the bar top.

"That's much better," Mrs. Corlis said happily. Now we can talk heart-to-heart, don't you think?" She beamed at me for a moment. "Why don't we drop the formalities, Mr. Boyd. Call me Beatrice." Her eyelashes fluttered extravagantly. "Now, what shall I call you?"

"Danny," I grunted.

"Ah, a Daniel come to judgment?" She giggled. "No, seriously, Danny, you've been a very naughty boy worrying poor Matthew the way you did! You deserve a spanking, you really do."

Michael gave her a drink, then handed me one with a derisive grin on his face. "That's real liquor," he sneered. "Watch you don't choke on it, punk!"

"Now, let me make a guess, Danny." Beatrice placed a finger under her plump chin coyly. "You went to Matthew and made all kinds of nasty threats and insinuations because you knew he'd call me right away, and you hoped I'd really believe you thought he was the boss, right?"

"It's your story, Beatrice," I said cautiously.

"That was meant to worry me into believing you were an unknown new element injected in the situation, right? Make me nervous—so nervous I'd jump at any kind of deal he offered me."

"He?" I queried.

"Oh, Danny—please!" She laughed joyously. "You can't honestly still be hoping I don't know Frankie Lomax is behind this?"

"Lomax?" I gurgled.

"He wants to panic me into a deal," she said composedly, "He has no chance, no chance at all. You tell him that for me, will you?"

"Lomax?" I croaked.

"Tell him it's a very simple situation, Danny." Her voice harshened suddenly. "He has one half, and I have the other. Neither of us can get any place until we put the two halves together. That makes sense surely?"

"It sure does." I had a sudden inspiration. "So what kind of a deal do you want, Beatrice?"

"A half is fifty per cent," she snapped. "That's the deal I want, fifty-fifty. It's perfectly reasonable."

I thought if I was sure I knew what she was talking about in the first place, I could come up with an intelligent answer. Meantime I could only stall and hope the sky fell in. The three of them watched me intently while I took a couple of slow sips from my glass, then lowered it carefully like it was sixteenth-century crystal.

"To you it's reasonable," I said, picking my words with the careful deliberation of an explosives expert who's forgotten which bombs are fused. "But to Frankie, it's not."

Tino moved across to the bar, made himself a drink, then lifted the glass and moved it in a gentle circle while he watched the swirling liquor with apparent absorption. "That Frankie Lomax," he said idly, "sometimes smart, sometimes not, huh? But always a punk!"

"So tell *him*," I said coldly.

"Let's not get hot about this, boys," Beatrice simpered. "I think when Danny tells him our proposition he'll see the sense of it."

"I don't buy that," Tino said lazily. "He's gotten cute already, now he's trying tricks, like scaring us with this Boyd here. If that don't work, maybe he'll think up some more tricks?"

"Like what?" Beatrice snapped.

"Like coming right in here and collecting our half for nothing," he suggested.

"Then I think we should convince him it would be most unwise to try, don't you?" she said.

"Yeah!" Michael said eagerly. "Like why don't we send this punk Boyd back to him in a barrel?"

"I don't think that would prove anything much," she said tersely. "What do you think, Tino?"

The dead eyes stared at the kid for a long moment,

NYMPH TO THE SLAUGHTER 63

then Tino shook his head slowly. "You got no brains, kid, none at all. All you got is the urge—beat up a guy real bad, put a couple of slugs into him and make it a real rub-out. That would make you feel a big man, huh?"

"It was only a suggestion!" the kid said in a sullen voice.

"But I'm right." Tino shook his head again sadly. "You got to lose the urge, kid, if you ever want to make a pro in this business. Pleasure don't count, only the percentages!" He turned around toward Beatrice, ignoring the kid. "You send Boyd back to Lomax dead, or in pieces, what does it prove? Nothing! It only makes Frankie figure the next time he wants to try, he won't come alone."

"Of course." Beatrice nodded her approval. "And it would be a shame to spoil that darling profile!" She pursed her lips at me for a moment, then giggled girlishly. "No, I've got a better idea. I think you should show Danny around the place before he leaves, Tino. Show him where we keep our half for safety, perhaps?"

"Okay," he said, nodding. "Mat hasn't let 'em loose yet?"

"You know he doesn't do anything until I tell him," she said easily. "It's quite safe."

"You want me along?" Michael asked hopefully.

"What for?" Tino sneered at him.

"Don't be unkind to the boy," Beatrice purred. "I want you to stay with me in any case, Michael. Keep me company while they're gone."

"Okay," he muttered.

She patted the arm of her chair confidently. "Fix me another drink and bring it with you over here, Micky. Your little girl's been so busy we haven't had a cozy chat all day, have we?"

For a moment a hunted look showed in the kid's eyes, then he busied himself making the drink.

"All right, Boyd." Tino pushed himself away from the bar. "Let's you and me make the two-bit tour, huh?"

I got up onto my feet as Michael took the drink across to Beatrice, then dutifully sat on the arm of her chair.

"You silly boy!" she whispered, one hand playfully ruffling his hair. "You mustn't be upset at anything Tino says! He's only trying to help you—isn't that right, Tino?"

"Sure." He knuckled the tip of his nose savagely. "Out the door, Boyd, and don't forget I'm right in back of you." He moved his gun in a small suggestive circle.

"There, you see?" Beatrice whispered. "Tino can teach you so much, Micky dear. The same way I'm teaching you a lot of things, and you don't mind that, do you?" She squeezed his biceps painfully, then giggled again.

I had a brief glimpse of the kid's face before Tino's gun in my back prodded me out into the hall, but it was long enough to see the glance of pure hate he bestowed on the top of Beatrice's head as she leaned it against his chest.

"Your little girl's had a hard day," she murmured contentedly, "but now her big strong Micky can make it better for her, h'mm?"

Then I was outside in the hall, with Tino giving me brief directions. We went through the house out onto the back porch, then across the immaculately kept lawn toward the huge kennels. I stopped when we reached the door and the gun barrel jabbed into my back.

"Open it," Tino gunted. "It's not locked."

The bloodcurdling savage ferocity of the sounds that hit my ears when I pushed open the door made my spine suddenly turn to water. For the first time in my life I knew the elemental terror of the primitive man who lurks deep in the primeval core of every civilized mind. For a timeless moment I was the naked Neanderthal gibbering his fear as the unknown beasts closed in for the kill.

NYMPH TO THE SLAUGHTER

"Go on!" Tino growled impatiently. "They can't get at you."

Reason came back into my mind warily, then was reassured by the logical premise that if Tino was lying, the beasts would get him, too. I stepped into the semi-gloom of the squat building, and cringed involuntarily as I saw the leaping bodies out of the corner of my eye. Then five powerful bodies slammed against reinforced wire mesh and I breathed again as they howled in frustrated fury.

"Pretty, aren't they?" Tino chuckled thinly.

I looked at narrow pointed heads, the sharp white teeth gleaming in wide-open slavering jaws, at long powerful legs that raised them to the height of a man's chest, and I shuddered.

"What in hell are they?"

"It's a good question," Tino said evenly. "Matthew Corlis is the only guy who can answer it. He bred and trained them and he's the only one who can handle the stinking things! Afghan hounds mostly, he says they are, but he won't tell what the rest is. Maybe it's better not to know, huh?"

"Corlis?" I said incredulously. "That little runt handles those—nightmares?"

"Maybe it's not so funny at that." Tino's voice was almost thoughtful. "You saw the kid back there? He can't wait to prove he's a big man, right? Maybe if you're made a runt like Corlis, you got to prove it worse than the kid even? In the house everybody else laughs right in his face. Out here with these things running loose he can laugh right back in everybody else's face."

"It makes sense," I agreed. "But I can understand the kid wanting to prove himself real fast—that way he could quit his pandering chores with the lady of the house!"

"He's a punk," Tino said seriously. "He's driving me half out of my mind! You and me, Boyd, we're pros, right?"

"What makes you say that?" I asked curiously.

"Ah, come on!" he snarled. "No amateur would pack

a Magnum for heat, you know that! They'd be too goddamned scared of blowing a big hole through themselves every time they holstered it."

"I guess you're right," I said modestly.

"Sure, I'm right," he said. "Lomax tells you to scare the hell out of Beatrice by making a big play you got nothing to do with him at all, right? So when Beatrice laughs right in your face, what do you do?—nothing! You don't get sore, you don't get yourself dead trying to be a big man, right? Because you're a pro. But the kid!" The frustration in his voice showed it was about to become a fixation. "Right off, the kid wants to send you back in a barrel. What's the percentage in that? But he don't even figure the percentages first!"

"Why don't you lose him, Tino?" I asked confidentially.

"You saw enough back in the house to know the answer!" he grated. "I got to wait until—ah, the hell with it!" He suddenly pointed down at the floor. "What's that, Boyd?"

"The floor," I said nervously.

"What's it made of?"

"Concrete."

"Look real close," he invited. "Underneath it is where Beatrice's fifty per cent of the deal is right now! You figure out a way to get to it?"

As far as I could see, the floor was an unbroken slab of concrete. "Not without a wrecking crew," I told him.

"You're goddamned right!" he said happily. "That's inches of reinforced concrete here. Okay, you've seen it all, let's get back to the house."

On our way in across the back porch, we met Matthew Corlis on the way out. He started nervously and skipped to one side with a crablike movement, his eyes rolling wildly while he tried hard to pretend we just weren't there at all.

"Tino's been showing me the results of your breeding, Mr. Corlis." I smiled at him politely.

NYMPH TO THE SLAUGHTER 67

"Oh?" Sudden interest shone in his eyes. "What did you—ah—think of them, Mr. Boyd?"

"They're certainly impressive," I said in the all-time understatement of D. Boyd's entire career.

"It took a lot of time and patience," he whispered happily. "But I think the results justified every minute."

"I'll go along with that," I told him, "they're—unique."

"Like my wife." He put a hand in front of his mouth suddenly, and I realized he'd made a joke. "What do you think of my—ah—wife, Mr. Boyd?"

"Repulsive," I said, without thinking.

The gun barrel sank painfully into my left kidney. "Cut out the cute comments, Boyd," Tino said irritably. "Where's the percentage?"

I slowly realized Corlis was staring at me, and the warm moist look in his eyes wasn't stunned hurt, but grateful admiration. "Mr. Boyd," he said huskily, "I wish I had—ah—said that!"

I walked past him into the house before Tino got real impatient and suddenly impaled me on that gun barrel. As we came down the front hall, the sound of a low sensual chuckle drifted through the open doorway.

"You silly boy!" Beatrice's voice purred throatily. "I'm only teasing. Why can't you relax and enjoy it?"

"Hold it!" Tino whispered fiercely in my ear. I stopped obediently and he raised his voice a couple of tones louder than necessary. "Okay, Boyd, back into the living room!"

When we entered the room, the kid was still sitting on the arm of her chair, his face flushed an angry red and his eyes burning with a complex mixture of shame and embarrassment. There was a faint pink showing in Beatrice's plump cheeks, and she breathed a little faster than normal through a half-open mouth.

"You're back already?" She primped her hair-do in a kind of automatic reflex. "Did Danny get to see everything?"

"Sure," Tino snapped. "It don't take that long."

Beatrice carefully tucked the hem of her dress down over her pudgy knees before she settled back into the chair and looked at me. Even then she couldn't keep her hands off the kid, her fingers kneading and pinching his arm the whole time.

"So go back to Frankie Lomax and tell him, Danny," she said finally. "If he ever thinks of trying to strongarm his way in here, he can forget it!"

"Sure," I said, nodding.

"You'd better itemize it for him," she added. "First there's the wall—those wires carry a couple of thousand volts, by the way. Then there's Tino and Micky, and another couple of boys who're out at the moment —and we mustn't forget the dogs, must we?"

"Nobody could ever forget the dogs, once they've seen them," I said fervently. "From here on I got my own built-in nightmare."

"That's fine." She smiled warmly. "Just tell Frankie, then. The deal is fifty-fifty, or nothing."

"Okay," I said dutifully. "Can I go now?"

"Why not?" she giggled. "Say goodbye to Danny like a good boy, Micky!"

"So long, punk!" the kid snarled. "Next time you won't get it so easy."

"If you stick to making the drinks, kid," I told him in an affectionate voice, "and try real hard not to run off at the mouth all the time, I figure you got a good chance of living until who knows?—maybe twenty-five, even."

"That's enough!" Beatrice snapped. "Tino—see Danny out, will you?"

"Yeah." He glared at me, then nodded toward the door. "You heard what she said!"

"You forgot something, Tino," I said.

"What?"

"The heat?"

"Yeah." He took my gun from the bar top, carefully emptied the slugs from it, then tossed it over. It wasn't that he didn't trust me, I thought wearily, he was just being careful, and the one-line chorus of Tino's favorite song fit neatly into place— "Because he's a pro."

I slid the empty Magnum back into the shoulder rig and turned toward the door.

"Just one thing more, Danny," Beatrice said easily. "You tell Frankie from me I'm in no hurry. I can afford to wait until I get what I want because there's no pressure. But he can't!"

"I'll tell him." I said tiredly.

Tino escorted me out to the car and watched me climb into the driver's seat before he holstered his gun. "I'll have the gates open by the time you reach them," he said. "For a guy who's got to give Frankie Lomax all that bad news when he gets back to town, you don't even look worried!"

"Like you said," I told him. "Sometimes smart—sometimes not—but always a punk."

"Yeah." He came up close to the side of the car and leaned his head inside the open window, so his face was only a foot away from mine. "I got a feeling about you, Boyd." He almost smiled. "You and me—" he held up two fingers pressed close together "—like that, huh?"

"Could be," I said.

"Sure, a couple of pros, watching the angles. You're a pretty smart guy, Boyd!"

"Thanks," I said humbly.

"Too smart to just work for Frankie Lomax much longer," he grated. "I got a feeling you're figuring the percentages real close, so you should know all the angles, right?"

"Right," I agreed.

"I got this feeling," he said slowly. "Don't ever come back here."

"Why not?"

"I don't explain it—it's something I feel like in my bones or something," he whispered. "You come back here, Boyd, I got to kill you."

I stared up into his face but even at that close range

all I got was my own taut reflection mirrored in his dead eyes.

"If I come back, Tino," I said softly. "I'll figure the percentages first!"

chapter 7

I came back across the Triboro Bridge around nine and felt thankful for my safe return to Gotham. Like every New Yorker knows, Manhattan is an island surrounded by primitive jungles that cunningly masquerade—under such innocent-sounding names as Long Island, New Jersey, Connecticut, and Westchester County—as civilized communities. But to the shrewd eye of the Manhattan dweller, the sordid truth is immediately apparent once he ventures into any of these regions.

The signs are infallible; the natives allow their grass and trees to grow wild at will, and their warriors exact tribute along their parkways to maintain their local chieftains in vulgar splendor. The unspeakable existence of their women who, instead of achieving their rightful place as civilized accessories to the male way of life, have become mere beasts of burden doomed to cultivate the miserable plots of land that surround their squat ugly dwellings. Worse, many of them die a horrible death, surrounded by work-shy domestic machinery, screaming piteously for the serviceman who will never come.

Knowing all this, I thought soberly, I had still deliberately ventured into the deep interior of Long Island! In a way I deserved the experience of Beatrice, to mention those five hounds of the Devil himself. What else would you expect in the heart of a primitive jungle but a bunch of real primitive primitives? For a moment I felt so secure now I was back in my own concrete canyons, I was almost tempted to take a walk through Central Park after dark. After all, some guy must have done it without getting mugged.

All that trail blazing had left me hungry so I stopped off at a small place on Second Avenue to eat. A rare steak, followed by a slab of Mother's mass-produced home-baked apple pie, took the edge off my hunger. I had a cigarette with my second cup of coffee and ran through the events of the last twenty-four hours in my mind. The composite picture of the profile's activities didn't exactly make me want to whoop with joy. Most of the time it felt like watching an old movie that kept jamming in the projector, so you had to see the same scene over and over again. It wasn't a real exciting scene either, just this guy, Boyd, walking around aimlessly with a gun in his back all the time.

A second cigarette with the third cup of coffee only made me more despondent about the whole bit. Now the mental picture changed and all I could see was myself being jammed into that projector by a whole bunch of different people in turn, who got real hilarious every time they watched me play that walk-around-with-a-gun-in-my-back scene. The hell with it, I thought finally, maybe it was time I started jamming a couple of other people into the projector. If I was real lucky the scenes they would play could come out real hilarious for me.

It was around a quarter after ten when I punched the doorbell of the Sutton Place penthouse, then waited with my brooding anger wrapped around me tight like a cocoon. I punched the doorbell again after a couple of minutes and still nothing happened. This

NYMPH TO THE SLAUGHTER

time I gave it about thirty seconds, then wedged the pointed end of my dime-store ball point pen into it, so it could ring all by itself until the battery ran out.

The door opened suddenly about six inches, and one wide brown eye glowered at me murderously. "Stop that racket!" she said fiercely, "or I'll call the super and have you thrown out of the building!"

I yanked the pen clear and the sudden silence collapsed around our ears like a winding sheet. "I have to see Osman Bey," I growled.

"He's gone to bed, come back in the morning!" she snapped, and I just got my foot wedged in the door a moment before she slammed it.

"It's urgent, so you'll have to get him up again," I said coldly.

"I wouldn't dare!" Selina gurgled. "I'm about ready to go to bed myself and he'd never——"

I put my shoulder against the door and heaved. There was one more frantic gurgle, then it swung wide open and at the same time Selina disappeared. It was impossible, I told myself as I stepped into the entrance hall; without even a puff of smoke she couldn't just vanish. Then an outraged snort from some place close to my feet made me look down, and there she was sprawled across the floor.

"Hit me again," Selina said bitterly. "There's no risk —I'm only a girl!"

"You should have let me in, honey," I said mildly, then I caught hold of her hands and pulled her to her feet.

I suddenly realized she really was just about ready for bed—the next stage had to be a pair of pajamas for sure. She wore a black satin bra that gave a truly awe-inspiring thrust to her wondrously full breasts, and matching panties with a froth of lace ruffles caressing the top of each thigh. At that moment Selina was Everyman's dream of desire, packed in the giant-sized frivolity carton.

"You look magnificent, honey," I said in humble tribute.

"You'll look real stupid when the super has you thrown out!" she panted.

"I give you a choice," I said generously. "Either you go wake up Osman Bey and tell him I'm here, or I'll do it!"

Alarm bells rang vigorously in her big brown eyes as she backed off a pace, then squinted at me nervously. "He'd kill me if you go in there," she muttered. "Maybe he'll kill me anyway. You wait right here, Boyd!" She swung around and walked quickly into the smaller vestibule that presumably led to the bedrooms.

She reappeared a couple of minutes later and walked right past me into the living room; a couple more minutes dragged by before she reappeared.

"He's getting dressed," she snapped. "You'd better wait in here."

I followed her into the living room and it didn't looked any different from when I'd first seen it the day before. The shades were still shut tight and the feeble light from one small table lamp made it gloomier still. The hookah waited mutely for any guy who liked to suck on his cigarette, then hang around waiting ten minutes for the smoke to arrive.

"He could be a while," the slave girl said gloomily. "He's not what you'd call a fast dresser—even when he's awake!"

"I'm just loaded with time right now," I told her.

"I figured that!" She sniffed. "You want a drink, or something?"

"Not that Turkish coffee!" I felt my stomach whimper at the thought.

"I mean liquor," she snapped.

"Some bourbon over ice?"

"I'll get it."

The ruffled lace ebbed and flowed gracefully with the slow majestic movements of her black satin rump, and the guy who figured Nature wasn't so wonderful was out of his tiny automated mind. I lit a cigarette and decided against squatting on one of those damned plush cushions that were scattered across the floor. After a little while I heard that delightful rustling sound of fragile lace brushing against fragile lace, then the slave girl returned with my drink.

I sipped it appreciatively while she stood with her arms folded under her magnificent bosom and watched me.

"He won't like it," she said finally. "You've never seen him when he's real mad, have you?"

"For me, he'll always look real mad whatever kind of mood he's in," I told her truthfully. "Mad like a nut, you know?"

"You just could get a nasty surprise!" There was an undercurrent of glee in her voice. "He's strong—you got no idea!"

"I could always jump out the window," I said.

"I'd like that," she said simply. "This is the twenty-fifth floor."

There was a faint slapping sound from the entrance hall, and by the time I'd identified it as the sound of Osman Bey's bare feet on the parquet flooring, he was already inside the room. His dark eyes gave me a brief glance, full of spawning murder, as he passed me in frigid silence. He stopped when he reached the hookah, and suddenly collapsed cross-legged onto the cushion beside it.

"I need coffee!" He spat the words at the slave girl, and her sudden nervous reaction resulted in a hopeless confusion of bouncing spheres. "I'll get it!" she squealed, and rushed out of the room, the spheres now rebounding upon the original confusion, rapidly changing it into erotic chaos.

"I always did feel for the guy who figured he'd never see anything so lovely as a tree," I said soberly. "He should have been here tonight!"

A faint hissing sound came from some place close to the hookah. "Did you drag me from my bed in the middle of the night to admire the physique of a slave girl I already own?" Osman Bey asked in a strangled voice.

"No, there was something else." I turned my head and took a good look at him.

Osman Bey hadn't changed any in twenty-four hours, either. Everything about him was the same. The long black hair was still oily and the tuft of beard faintly ridiculous; he even wore the same blue silk shirt over his bulging paunch and the same bilious-green pants tight across his thighs. Silver lacquer still gleamed dully whenever he wriggled his toes.

"I have had an unbearable day!" he said vehemently. "A day to torment the soul of a saint! Four hours of viperous interrogation and degrading physical torture at the hands of my once-revered partner, Abdul Murad—may camels defile the burial places of his ancestors! When he left to visit your office, I fled trembling into the bowels of the city to escape his unjust wrath. For hours I trudged the burning streets beneath the pitiless sun, until night came and I returned exhausted to my abode, seeking the sweet sanctuary of sleep, and for a little time, forgetfulness."

His fat cheeks quivered with fury. "Then you come storming at my door, ringing a thousand bells, like some idiot peddler with no wares to sell! You drag me from my merciful slumbers and force me back into the nightmare world of the living—for what?"

"Now Abdul Murad's in town, I figured you'd be ever more interested to hear what progress I've made so far," I told him.

"May Allah spit on your shaven head throughout eternity!" he said, nearly choking. "Why cannot it wait until morning!"

"Because too much is happening," I snarled. "Too much has happened to me already."

Selina crept back into the room with all curves subdued, and offered him his coffee. He snatched the cup from her hands and scowled thunderously at her.

"You," he grated. "You hoarder of flesh! You useless bovine idiot! You—you let him in! "His eyes rolled toward the ceiling in a beseeching gesture. "May Allah grant you spend eternity sitting on a

NYMPH TO THE SLAUGHTER

sharp-pointed spear with a host of starving eunuchs, all armed with razor-edged daggers, clustered at your feet eagerly awaiting the moment when you topple."

The slave girl moaned in terror, then backed away from him so fast she overbalanced and fell sprawling onto the floor. Without even a split second's hesitation, she flipped over onto her stomach and crawled toward the door at an incredible speed.

"Hold it, Selina!" I yelled.

Her black satin rump twitched painfully, then she slowed down to a reluctant stop.

"She belongs to me, D. Boyd!" Osman Bey said thickly. "It is for me to say when she goes and when she stays. Now, I say she goes!"

"She stays," I growled. "I want her to hear this."

"You—" he spluttered. "You question my commands?"

"Ah, shut up and drink your coffee!" I yelled at him. "If you don't stop talking and start listening, we'll be here all night."

For a moment there, I figured the dark eyes would pop clean out of his head. Then he made a curious gobbling noise deep in his throat. "I will listen!" he said thinly. "After that, I may strike you dead!"

"Leave us face that problem when the time comes," I pleaded. "Selina—do me a favor and get up on your feet. The way you are right now you look like a confused camel train!"

The slave girl scrambled quickly onto her feet and stood with her hands clasped in front of her and her head bowed submissively.

I told them what had happened the previous night from the time I got into Leila Zenta's dressing room at the Ottoman Club. How Frankie Lomax had been there, and refused to believe that I was working for Osman Bey, and insisted it was Corlis who had sent me there.

"Corlis?" Osman Bey tugged his beard gently. "Who is this Corlis?"

"I'll get around to that," I said coldly. "It's important I tell it in sequence."

"As you wish," he said in a fretful voice. "It was just that I do not like things I do not understand."

"I know just how you feel," I told him. "Stay with it and get more confused along with me!"

I continued the story—how Julie Kern had appeared, and his threats about what The Man would do to Lomax if he didn't either deliver the package or pay the cash value of it within the next forty-eight hours. How I'd managed to grab Lomax's gun, and Leila had volunteered to prove they didn't have Marta Murad held prisoner by showing me their prisoner. And when we got into the cellar we'd found the body of a little fat guy who couldn't have been dead for very long before we arrived.

I skipped over the detail of how I'd gotten out of the club, and jumped forward to my lunch-time meeting with Corlis and the appointment at his Long Island home. It took a long time to wade through the detail of that visit—the people I'd met, my late discovery that Beatrice—Mrs. and not Mr.—Corlis was the brains of the outfit. Then her assumption that I was one of Lomax's hoods, and her offer of a deal—she had half and Lomax had half—and she wanted 50 per cent of the take before she'd agree to putting both halves together. Finally a short, sharp description of how well the house was protected, including the hounds and all, wrapped it up.

Osman Bey stared at me blankly, one hand caressing his beard with gentle care. Selina still stood in the exact position she'd adopted before I started my story, her hands clasped in front of her and her head bowed.

"It—it is amazing, D. Boyd," Osman Bey said in a hushed voice. "An incredible story—but obviously true! To invent such a tale would stagger the imagination. You have worked hard in my service and I commend you for it—but my mind reels at the implications! Tell me, what have you deduced?"

"A couple of things," I told him. "You don't believe

NYMPH TO THE SLAUGHTER 79

in coincidence if you've got a nasty suspicious mind the way I have."

"Coincidence?" He frowned worriedly. "What was coincidence, D. Boyd?"

"The timing," I grunted. "There was just time enough for Frankie Lomax to start getting real rough with me, from the time I walked into Leila's dressing room to the time Julie Kern made his entrance."

"I am still confused," Bey muttered. "Explain it more, please?"

"Kern walked in there at the exactly right psychological moment," I went on. "It made my presence there an embarrassment to Lomax so he was at a disadvantage from the start. Then Julie skilfully put on the pressure, showing his open contempt for Frankie while he did it. By the time he'd finished I figure Lomax had forgotten I even existed. So taking his gun was like taking candy from a kid. The only guy who could have stopped me was Julie himself—but he didn't."

"That is the coincidence?"

"Part of it," I said patiently. "Then Julie let me lock him in the closet along with Lomax, and even that was out of character. The coincidence is, like I said before, in the timing. I don't believe Julie Kern just happened to walk in there at that moment, or that he happened to goad Lomax the way he did, either."

Osman Bey nodded slowly. "Now, I think it comes clear to me, this coincidence."

"Who knew I was going to the Ottoman Club last night to try and get some information out of Leila Zenta?"

He thought about it for a moment, then his fat cheeks shook with indignation. "Are you accusing me of—"

"Not you," I snarled, "and not me, either. There was only one other person in the room, remember?"

"You mean—" His bulging eyes slowly transferred their gaze from my face to the slave girl's bowed head.

"Selina, who else?" I agreed.

"Is it possible?" Bey nearly choked on his words. "I have been clasping a traitor to my bosom?"

I suppressed the thought that where bosoms were concerned, if anyone did any clasping to, it wouldn't be Osman Bey.

"I can almost paint a picture," I said flatly. "During your liaison with Leila Zenta you were a little indiscreet, like you told me. You mentioned to her you had your own private pipeline from Europe to New York, for the kind of goods that couldn't face up to a customs inspection. Leila passed on the information to her boy friend, Frankie Lomax. Then later, Julie Kern tells Lomax he needs a safe pipeline for a most important package his boss is sending from Europe. Lomax sees the chance of a quick profit, says he can give him one that's foolproof. Then Frankie makes a deal with you which gives him something off the top, then introduces you to Julie Kern, the client, right?"

"Right." Bey nodded miserably. "The start of all my troubles!"

"Julie knows the package contains diamonds worth a couple of hundred grand," I continued. "He figures Lomax is only a small-time punk who wouldn't dare cross him on the deal, but then Lomax is only the middleman, anyway. You're the guy who's going to handle the operation, and about you he knows nothing. So Julie figures he wants somebody real close to you the whole time—somebody who can report your every move. His problem is how to put somebody that close without arousing your suspicions, right?

"So he asks around discreetly and Leila tells him your big weakness is dancing girls, with belly dancers rating the jackpot. It wouldn't be any problem to get into a friendly card game with you, and stack the deck so he lost a thousand dollars. Then pull a big act about how he's temporarily short of money, but he'll give you something else instead—like this broad who's crazy to be a belly dancer?"

"A viper cradled to my bosom!" Bey said thickly.

NYMPH TO THE SLAUGHTER

Selina's head lifted sharply, revealing the real worried look on her face. "Now look, boys"—her voice was shaking—"we don't want to jump to any wrong conclusions, do we?"

"All you have to do, honey, is jump in with the right answers to some questions," I said gently. "Like, who is 'The Man' Julie keeps talking about?"

"I don't know," she said in a flat voice.

I grabbed her wrist and twisted it hard so she was forced down onto her knees in front of me, her arm bent painfully behind her back.

"Selina, honey," I said cheerfully, "this doesn't hurt me one little bit. I want you should remember that—even if I have to twist your arm clean out of its socket, I'll feel no pain at all."

"Don't," she whimpered. "Please don't."

"All you got to do is answer the questions," I grated. "So let's start over, huh?" Who is The 'Man'?"

"Big Max," a metallic voice from the doorway answered my question. "Big Max Morel, Boyd."

"Thanks, Julie," I said stiffly.

"Now, let go the kid's arm before I get rough!"

Julie Kern came into the room, the gun fitting his hand like it had been specially tailored by a master craftsman—and maybe it had, like the rest of his personal possessions. I let go of Selina's wrist and she stood up again, massaging it gently, making a big production out of it like I'd hurt it real bad.

"You okay, kid?" Kern asked.

"He hurt me, Julie!" There was a momentary flash of fiendish glee in her innocent brown eyes as she glanced at me before turning toward Kern. "He hurt me real bad, Julie!" she sobbed in a little-girl-betrayed kind of voice. "I think maybe there's something—broken—inside.

The puckered white scar that drew the corner of his mouth down into a permanent snarl seemed to throb gently. "Take it easy, kid," he whispered. "I'll even the score, and that's a promise!"

"Make it real good—for me, huh, Julie?" she whispered eagerly.

"Yeah." Kern looked at Osman Bey menacingly. "Listen, you fat old goat! Selina stays here. I'm going out for a while, but I'll be back. If you've even looked at her I'll—"

"No, please!" Bey shrieked. "I swear on the Koran that I will not harm her in any way—I give you my word—I—"

"I'll be back," Julie repeated. "Okay, Boyd. Let's have the gun—like real slow, huh?"

"Sure," I said. "But it's empty."

"I'll believe it after I've looked," he grunted. "Drop it on the floor, then kick it over to the girl."

I did like he said, and as the gun skittered across the floor toward her, Selina bent down eagerly and snatched it up.

"Watch it, honey," I said in an overanxious voice. "That was your bad wrist. You know? The one with maybe something—broken—inside?"

Her cheeks burned a dull red color, which was reflected in the burning fury of her eyes. "You—" She took a deep breath. "I'd like to—"

"Some other time, baby," Kern snapped. "Let's go, Boyd."

While we stood waiting for the elevator, I wondered why there seemed an almost overpowering familiarity about everything that had happened from the time Julie Kern appeared on the scene. Then I suddenly realized the answer. I'd been jammed right back into that projector and was playing that whole dreary bit all over again—the scene where I walk around with a gun in my back.

chapter 8

Julie Kern had a car parked around the corner from the apartment building, and a driver waiting inside it, which was even more depressing. He said something in a low voice that I couldn't catch to the driver, then bundled me into the back seat and sat beside me. The car moved out from the curb at a leisurely pace, and it would have been real nice to relax, sit back, and enjoy it.

"Julie," I said, trying hard to make it sound friendly. "You got plans for me, I guess?"

"I got plans for you, Boyd."

"You mind if I ask what? Or is it a big military secret?"

"I'd enjoy discussing them with you, Boyd," he almost purred. "Why don't we start with the basic problem? You served your purpose and now I don't need you any more. To be real honest, just having you around could be an embarrassment. What I wanted to do was give you back to the Indians but they got their pride—so then I figured out the next best thing."

"I know I'm not about to like it," I said bleakly. "But tell me, anyway."

"It got to be a real problem," he purred. "Let's face it, Boyd. Who needs a two-bit private eye, even as a gift?"

"I have a little black book in my apartment," I said hopefully. "Why don't we go up there and call the girls in alphabetical order? I'm sure one of them would want me—well, for a weekend anyway—"

"Relax," he said easily. "I solved the whole problem, when I remembered the names of the two people who'd really appreciate you as a gift. You with me, Boyd?"

"I got a nasty feeling I'm way ahead of you," I snarled. "But it's your punch line."

"Frankie Lomax and Leila Zenta!" he said almost happily. "After the way you handled him last night—and the way you handled his dame—boy! They sure love you. You should see how they react when your name's mentioned."

I eased the pack of cigarettes carefully out of my pocket and put one in my mouth. Julie struck a match for me, and as the flame flared I thought for one unbelievable moment there was a smile on his face.

"How do you like that, Boyd?" he prodded. "We're on our way to the Ottoman Club right now."

"Julie," I said soberly, "who did that corpse in the cellar belong to?"

"Corpse? What corpse?"

"You know what corpse," I grunted. "I bet you know that cellar door's made of steel too, with a combination lock on the outside."

"So?"

"So Leila told me on the way down how Frankie figured the combination was the best way to protect anything he had in the cellar. Only three or four people had the combination, so if anything was stolen, it wouldn't be hard for Lomax to figure out just who the thief was."

"You keep running off at the mouth all the time, but you don't say anything!" he grated.

"I want to be sure you got the picture right, Julie,"

I said sincerely. "Whoever made that corpse down there last night had to know the combination to get in there. Leila says three or four at most, all of them would have to be working for Lomax. That kind of ensures the corpse was made on Frankie's orders, doesn't it?"

"Who cares?" he grunted. "What difference does it make to you?"

"I saw the body," I said gently. "Even if they've gotten rid of it by now, I'm a witness who can testify I saw the body in that cellar. You think Frankie will let me walk around with that tucked inside my head, if you give him the chance of putting me on ice permanently?"

"So Lomax knocks off a two-bit private eye," he sneered thinly. "I weep!"

"Maybe you don't," I told him. "My secretary weeps, my files weep, a couple of close contacts in the same line of business, they maybe weep a little, too. Then all them ask the same question: What was Danny doing he should get himself knocked off? The funny thing is they all get the same answer—he was working for a guy named Osman Bey who figured his partner's daughter was kidnaped around five days back—and so on. Would you want that, Julie?"

"Ah, shut up!" he snarled. "I'm thinking."

"Big Max Morel," I said in an apologetic voice. "Would he want that?"

He leaned forward and spoke to the driver. "Skip the Ottoman Club. Let's just cruise around through the park for a while."

"Big Max Morel?" I said reflectively. "He was one of the biggest, huh?"

"They don't come no bigger than Big Max," Julie snapped.

"He was deported—three years back?"

"Close enough."

"And now he runs the organization by long distance from Europe—through you?"

"When Big Max said goodbye, the Syndicate carved

up the organization," he said tersely. "All by agreement, of course. They gave Max a couple of big operations, one in Italy and the other in the south of France. They let him keep a couple of medium-sized operations right here on the East Coast, and I run them for him. That's all there is to it."

"You run them for him?" I sounded impressed. "Big Max must have a lot of faith in you, Julie!"

"Sure, we worked together ten years before he left."

"With a relationship like that, I guess losing a couple of hundred grand in diamonds wouldn't mean a thing, huh?"

I felt his body stiffen beside my mine and sucked in my stomach tight, not breathing for a moment.

"Don't push it any more, Boyd," he whispered harshly. "Or I'll let you have it right now!"

"You got me wrong, Julie," I said earnestly. "I'm trying to make a point."

"You already made it!"

"Look," I said in a real respectful tone of voice, "you want the diamonds back. My client, the fat little creep, Osman Bey—he wants the diamonds and the girl. Lomax wants the diamonds. I guess the girl's father just wants her. We all want the same thing basically. If Lomax gets the ice he'll turn it over to you to take the heat off. If I get it, I give it to my client, and he'll turn it over to you for the same reason. What the hell are we fighting about?"

For what seemed a hell of a long time Kern just sat huddled beside me on the back seat, without either saying a word or moving a muscle. The car still moved leisurely, through the Park out on 66th, then back down Broadway.

Right in the middle of all the flashing neon, Kern suddenly sat up straight and eased his hand inside his coat. Three years of my life had been chopped away before he finally withdrew his hand, and it came out holding a pack of cigarettes. I took one gratefully and he struck another match for me.

NYMPH TO THE SLAUGHTER 87

"You got some ideas, Danny?" For the first time I thought I detected a degree of warmth in his voice.

"Some," I said, "but they need a lot more work. The big thing it seems to me is that we don't rush it. We could blow the whole thing for good by making a stampede out of it, you agree?"

"Yeah." He stared out at the theater crowd flooding the sidewalks on either side of us for a few seconds. "You think about it some more, Danny, and we'll talk sometime tomorrow. I'll call your office maybe late in the afternoon."

"Fine," I said.

"Can we drop you any place?"

"Sure, my apartment," I said gratefully. "If you don't mind backtracking uptown again. I'm on Central Park West." I gave him the number.

He leaned forward for a moment and told the driver, then relaxed back into the seat. "That Selina!" There was no expression in his voice at all. "The way she hammed up that itty-bitty arm-twisting bit, hey? I bet she's still hoping I'll bring her back your head in a bucket!"

"I'll believe it," I said.

He paused deliberately. "If you want, I'll have her delivered to your apartment in a half hour?" The scar down one side of his mouth twitched suddenly. "She bruises real easy," he added softly, "but then there's such a lot of Selina to bruise!"

"No, thanks all the same," I told him. "I've had a hard day already—but I'd appreciate it if I could have my gun back."

"Sure, I'll have Joe—" he nodded toward the driver, "—bring it right over after we've dropped you."

Ten minutes later the car stopped right outside my own apartment block. I watched it pull away from the curb and lost sight of it in the traffic a couple of blocks off. Even then I didn't have the confidence to convince myself that the sidewalk under my feet was real and the apartment building was where I lived. Subconsciously I was waiting for the next guy along to jam me into that projector, so I could automatically act out that gun-in-the-back routine.

As soon as I got into the apartment, I made myself the Boyd bourbon special. The whole art is in the mixing—you take a highball glass and fill it to the rim with neat bourbon, then the skill comes in floating a couple of ice cubes onto the surface without spilling one drop of bourbon. This was one time I cheated a little and just didn't bother with the ice cubes.

The buzzer sounded about the same time I reached the bottom inch of liquor in the glass. Outside was Joe—I guessed—I never got to see anything but his back in the car.

"Mr. Kern said to give you this." He handed me a brown paper package.

"Thanks," I told him.

"And he said if you want to change your mind about the other package, it would be no trouble to send it over gift-wrapped in black satin."

"Thanks, but no thanks," I said.

"Whatever you say, Mr. Boyd."

I closed the door in back of him, wondering if Selina ever felt she had real job security, then took the package into the living room. It was the Magnum, of course, and I felt glad to get it back, while I tried hard not to remember it was the second time that day I'd had to politely *ask* for it back. There was a carton of shells in the dresser, I remembered, and now seemed a good time to reload the gun before something else happened, so I headed toward the bedroom.

Maybe the Prince did get a real boot out of suddenly seeing Sleeping Beauty stretched out in front of his eyes, but I'm not convinced. I figure the chances are the sudden shock of finding her unexpectedly like that hit him a painful blow right under the heart—and for the next couple of minutes he thought the hell with Sleeping Beauty—was that a coronary or wasn't it?

The pain wore off after the first couple of minutes,

and I dared to think it hadn't been a coronary after all. Sleeping Beauty was still stretched out on my bed, sleeping peacefully, her conical hair-do slightly mussed so that a couple of blonde strands strayed around the curve of her cheek. The tight skirt had hiked up on one side, exposing a perilous length of firmly rounded thigh. My pulse accelerated alarmingly, showing a reckless disregard for the near-coronary of a few minutes before.

I walked across to the bed, grabbed her shoulder, and shook it vigorously. She smiled vaguely without opening her eyes, so I shook her again with even greater vigor.

"Oh, sure," she murmured sleepily. "I bet he's the biggest lecher this side of the Hudson, but that crazy profile!" Her gurgling laugh sounded like a censor's death knell. What the hell, I figured amiably, I could wake her any time—and maybe there was more to come about the profile.

"H'mmm," she sighed, and the sound was a complete pagan dictionary in itself, bound and indexed. "It's the wildest thing you ever saw! Like hilarous, you know? It kind of slopes downwards and out from his hairline, and upwards and out from his chin, and meets at the tip of his nose—well, I say tip, but I guess it's more bulbous!—so whenever he turns his head sideways it looks like a tipped-over isosceles triangle!" She gurgled with obscene laughter.

"Wake up, you myopic strumpet!" I yelled savagely, and shook her like she was a rug that hadn't been moved in the last fifteen years.

"H'mmm," she yawned louder this time but that was all. "His chin? Depends which one you're talking about—no, I'd prefer not to discuss his mouth if you don't mind, but I'll give you a one-word clue—yes—fleshy!"

I watched closely while I shook her shoulder again and there was a discernible twitch in her right eyelid, then the long lashes parted cautiously a millimeter at a time. It was the kind of game two could play, I figured, and I concentrated on placing the ultimate expression of leering naked lust onto my face, before she got that eye open enough to sneak another look to see how I was reacting to her monologue. Amazingly enough, I got the ultimate in that kind of expression onto my face with hardly any effort at all.

"If that won't wake her, nothing will," I muttered feverishly. "So I can strip off her clothes first." I chuckled evilly. "Get me some real juicy flash-bulb studies, and make me a fortune out of selling prints to all those Broadway novelty shops! Then I could—"

Both eyes opened wide and I felt the fiery stare of her cobalt-blue eyes. "Enough, Danny Boyd," she said crisply.

"Well," I said defensively, "look at the way you put me on, pretending to talk in your sleep and all?"

"Touché!" She sat up and yawned, stretching her arms above her head luxuriantly. "That's the best sleep I've had in weeks!"

"You're some kidder!" I said carefully. "All that jazz about the profile, it was real wild, hey?"

"No," she said lightly, "it was the stone cold truth —only I was anticipating a little, say five years?"

I had to admit my laugh had a hollow sound even to my own ears. "Can't you just see me pedaling those flash-bulb pix up and down Broadway?" I chuckled ironically. "Some fat little guy with a big sneer on his face saying, 'A dime a dozen for them? Mister, are you out of your mind?'"

"Hah!" Kitty Torrence said disdainfully. "The difference between us, Mr. Boyd, is that I've *seen* your profile!"

"Yeah," I said gloomily, "I hadn't thought about that aspect. Well"—I brightened suddenly—"fair is fair, right? Now I've shown you my profile from all angles, how about you showing me—"

She shook her lovely blonde head in mock amazement. "I have to say one thing for this boy," she announced to an imaginary auditorium. "He's a tryer! Long after the race is over and the stadium's closed

NYMPH TO THE SLAUGHTER 91

up for the night, who is the lone figure still toiling around the track? Non other than—"

"Hey!" I growled. "You sidetracked me. How the hell did you get in here?"

"I told the doorman I was your little sister just off the train from Brushy, North Carolina, and I had no place else to go."

"And he let you in on the strength of a corny old—"

"No," she corrected me. "He was very rude and said it was dames like me that gave good apartment buildings like this a bad reputation."

"What then?"

"I apologized and said it was my corny sense of humor, and the truth of it was the Young Executives League's big sweepstake was drawn late this afternoon and you held the winning ticket. Then I kind of stroked his lapels a little and appealed to his sense of chivalry, you know? I asked him straight out what can a first prize in a big sweepstake do about the delivery problem? I couldn't go to Macy's or Gimbel's and ask them to gift-wrap me and send me through the mails, could I? And he said, 'Honey! I'll deliver you myself!' and he did!"

A couple of seconds later I remembered my mouth was hanging wide open, and I closed it with a sharp clicking noise.

"I'd love to believe I'm irresistible, but you're such a cynical-type blonde," I said cautiously. "You had a reason for coming up here, or you just felt tired and wanted to lie down?"

"Oh!" She clapped her hand over her mouth. "Isn't that dreadful, Danny? I almost forgot! It was all Mr. Corlis's idea."

"Corlis?"

"He called me at my apartment around eight-thirty tonight—it was all terribly mysterious. A matter of life and death, he said, and would I contact that Mr. Boyd I overstayed my lunch hour with today, immediately, and deliver a message."

"What was the message?" I asked.

Kitty closed her eyes for a moment. "I have to be sure and get it exactly right because it doesn't make any sense, anyway. Mr. Corlis said, 'Tell your Mr. Boyd it can be done from the beach if you watch out for trip-wires close to the top.' It sounds like the punch line of a very doubtful story to me. Does it make any sense to you?"

"Yeah," I said, nodding. "Any more?"

"There's more." She closed her eyes again and concentrated for a moment. "Something like, 'Maybe I can take care of the hounds while he finds some place to hang his coat.' Does it still make sense, Danny?"

"The first bit about the dogs does," I muttered, "but that 'while he finds someplace to hang his coat.' What the hell is that supposed to mean?"

"Don't ask me! After he said it, Mr. Corlis kind of giggled and said you'd work it out if you were as smart as he thought you were, and only half as smart as you thought you were!"

"Thanks a bunch, Mr. Corlis!" I grunted.

She swung her long legs off the bed, got onto her feet, and sauntered over to the mirror. I heard a sudden shriek of despair. "Danny Boyd, get out of here!" she wailed. "I look like Dracula's daughter, exhumed after forty years in the tomb without one single pint of fresh blood in my veins all that time!"

"I'll make us a drink?" I suggested.

"Do anything that'll keep you busy some place outside this room!" she pleaded.

I started toward the living room at a gentle trot, figuring the quicker I was out of the bedroom the better Kitty would like it, and a moment later I plunged heavily to the floor as my foot collided with a heavy, unyielding object I knew just shouldn't have been there in the first place.

"Clumsy!" Kitty said in a tart voice.

If my bones weren't all broken, I knew damn well they'd been rearranged in a completely new pattern which might well look simply grotesque, so I took my time about staggering back onto my feet.

"Do I look any different to you?" I asked shakily.

"No, unfortunately!" she snapped. "What do your friends have to do to get you to leave when the party's over? Call a fire truck?"

"I didn't see—" I looked at the object of my downfall and was suddenly deprived of speech. "What"—I finally managed to manipulate my vocal chords again—"in the name of sanity is that?"

"Oh, that?" There was a faintly nervous edge to Kitty's voice. "That's my purse."

"Purse?" I said, strictly falsetto. "It looks more like a cabin trunk! Did the doorman carry that up in one hand, and you in the other?"

"I like a big purse," she muttered indistinctly. "All the things a girl needs to carry around with her these days. It takes a big purse—"

"Oh, sure," I said. "A girl never knows when she could be marooned in Times Square for six months, and it would be too embarrassing if she had to wear the same outfit twice!"

"Everything's big these days," Kitty mumbled on doggedly, "I've always used size thirty-two handkerchiefs—and then I smoke king-sized cigarettes—and a compact compact is worse than useless—and—Danny Boyd, will you please get the hell out of here!"

Back in the living room I made a real fast reconnaissance, pulling a drape further across a window here—switching out an unnecessary lamp there—until the room looked real cozy even if you couldn't see very well. I made a batch of brandy alexanders and set it up with the appropriate glasses on a coffee table in front of the couch, then sat down and waited expectantly.

Maybe twenty minutes later I heard the click as the bedroom door opened, and a moment later an immaculate, conical-shaped blonde hair-do peeked around the edge of the door.

"Danny Boyd," she said in a small voice. "Do you know what time it is?"

"Why?" I said bitterly. "Are we just entering harbor, or something?"

"It's almost two A.M.," she said.

"You should worry," I growled, "you've had almost a full night's sleep already!"

"Maybe I should be leaving?"

That hideous crunching sound, I realized a moment later, was my own teeth busy grinding each other to powder.

"Well," I said, grimacing savagely. "It's been a wonderful evening, Miss Torrence, and I can only say I've had a real ball. Of course, it was kind of lonely —just me, I mean—but I never lost a single game of checkers or—"

"Now you're mad at me for some reason?" she whispered dolefully.

"It's just that I'd kind of planned on us having a little time together, like the two of us in the same room," I snarled. "I even made us a batch of brandy alexanders to go along with the conversation!"

"Oh!" There was a sudden lilt in her voice. "Then you don't want me to go home?"

"Are you out of your mind?" I yelped.

"Well, you got so mad about that overnight case of mine—the one you tripped over, remember?—that I thought you were giving me what's politely known as a broad hint!"

"I stubbed my toe," I explained carefully. "I probably dislocated my spine, wrenched my left knee, and bent five ribs on each side, when I fell over the damned thing. I was *mad*."

"Oh?" she said softly. "But you're not mad at me any more?"

"Definitely not!"

"And you don't think I should go home?"

"Absolutely not!"

"I'm so glad!" she said happily. "I would have felt such a fool looking for a cab like this!"

She suddenly emerged from the bedroom and kind of floated toward the couch. I would have said something but my tongue had suddenly welded itself to the roof of my mouth. She wore something that had obviously been designed for sleeping in—during the summer months—in a tropical climate—where even a quarter-ounce of unnecessary weight could mean a disturbed night's rest. It was made—what there was of it—from gossamer-fine sheer nylon that clung to her like a summer morning's mist.

For a breathtaking moment she floated above the couch, then gently came to rest real close beside me. At that range I could see it was a two-piece outfit, and not completely transparent, although the 10 per cent that wasn't didn't really matter. The top was just long enough to reach her hips and clung tight enough to reveal the coral-pointed tips of her small but perfectly rounded breasts. The other half of the outfit was a pair of bikini-sized pants that fit snug around the tops of her thighs, then climbed boldly toward her waist, and suddenly quit when they'd covered maybe the first four inches of her hips. I could sympathize —a vertical climb over an outthrusting curve takes a hell of a lot of nerve.

"You approve?" she asked in a small voice.

"Approve?" I gurgled. "It's magnificent! It's just a shame it has to get so close to you, it suffers by comparison."

A faintly luminous cobalt-blue gleam seemed to radiate from her elfin face. "I wouldn't want to be unfair, Danny. You really think it is unfair, having it so close to me all the time?"

"Spun from moonbeams, cobwebs, and mountain mist," I said sadly, "as it obviously has been, it still can't compare with your own flawless beauty, Kitty. Yes, I have to say it, you are being unfair!"

That provocative lower lip of hers protruded alarmingly, and her low gurgling laugh would have made Don Juan stop and think for a moment. "Then pour me a drink, Danny, while I stop being unfair!"

The shaker and the glass chattered like a couple of lonely suburban housewifes, forcing me to concentrate real hard on pouring the drink. I turned toward her with the glass in my hand, and almost spilled the contents straight into my own lap. She wasn't being unfair anymore and the gossamer outfit was no longer close to her own beauty, it had simply disappeared.

Under the muted glowing warmth of the solitary lamp, her body was a mosaic pattern of delight, fashioned by some lyric poet in tones and shades of porcelain, amber, and coral. She took the glass from my hand, clasping it firmly between her own two hands, then raised it to her lips and sipped delicately.

"It's just right, Danny," she whispered. "Why don't you stop all the clocks now? I don't want it ever to be morning!"

"You want to hear a funny story?" I asked her. "Earlier tonight somebody offered me a belly dancer, gift-wrapped in black satin, and I declined the offer! That was the smartest thing I ever did in my whole life!"

"Danny Boyd!" Her voice was warm with tolerant amusement. "It's a wild Irish imagination you have—and I'm hoping it has a practical side to it, and all!"

"That's a challenge I can't resist," I said happily.

"Danny?"

"Huh?"

"I haven't finished my drink yet."

"I'm sorry, honey. I didn't know you wanted to finish it."

"Isn't that the funniest thing? Suddenly, I don't, either!"

chapter 9

Across the breakfast table the conical hair-do was now vertical; that is, it started from the crown of her head, and hung down either side of her elfin face.

"I must look like the wrath of something," Kitty said anxiously.

"You look incredibly beautiful and intensely desirable," I told her truthfully. "The way any girl who sits down to breakfast wearing only a pair of leopard-print panties and bra *should* look!"

"You're cute, Danny," she said fondly. "Insatiable, too."

"What time is it?"

She glanced at the minute watch on her wrist and moaned softly. "Ten-thirty, and I'm lolling about here half naked, eating breakfast! Mr. Corlis will fire me for sure!"

"Not when you tell him what a tough time you had delivering his message to me," I said reassuringly. "Does that job mean so much to you, Kitty?"

"Well—" she shrugged expressively "—it's the only one I've got."

Her coffee was better than mine would ever be, so I

sneaked a third cup while she wasn't looking. I watched her lower lip unconsciously protrude another quarter-inch, while she was deep in thought.

"Don't forget our date tonight," I reminded her. "Eight, sharp!"

"You know something, Danny?" she frowned at me seriously. "I only met you yesterday at lunch-time, when you apparently frightened poor little Mr. Corlis out of his skin almost. Then the same evening he called, asked me to give you that nut-language message and said it was a matter of life and death. And last night, the first time you walked into the bedroom, you were carrying a gun. It suddenly occurs to me I have no idea how you earn your living—although I've already presumed you're not with the public health board?"

"I'm Danny Boyd, of Boyd Enterprises," I said and grinned. "Which is a fancy name for a private detective."

"Are you working on a case right now where Mr. Corlis is involved?" she asked eagerly.

"He's involved," I said, "but I don't think it's his own idea."

"How about that friend of yours who sells Mr. Corlis some of his junk? Is he involved?"

"Huh?" I said.

"You know—the one with Arabian Nights name— Osman Bey?"

I stared at her dully for a few seconds. "I'd forgotten about that," I muttered. "I'm glad you reminded me."

"Service is our motto!" She leaped up from the table —a gazelle in leopard's clothing—and ran for the bedroom. "If I'm not there before he wants to go to lunch, I know he'll fire me for sure!" she called over her shoulder.

It was like she'd pushed a button inside my head and a tape automatically replayed. I listened to myself recounting the events of twenty-four hours to a hysterical Osman Bey and a cowering king sized slave girl. "You don't believe in coincidence if you've got a nasty suspicious mind the way I have," the tinny replica of my own voice said smugly. And later, "The timing ... I don't believe Julie Kern just happened to walk in there at that moment ..."

I must have been punchy with that gun-in-the-back routine, I thought savagely. That wry little analogy, born out of self-pity, about being jammed back into the projector by a whole bunch of different people in turn, was so close to the truth it didn't matter. And you bet they got hilarious every time they watched me play the same scene over and over. They were probably still laughing hilariously right now!

A fully dressed Kitty went flying past me on her way toward the front door. " 'Bye, Danny," she called breathlessly. "I love you madly and I'll see you tonight at eight. Can we make it here, because I didn't have time to pack my things in the cabin trunk yet?"

"It's fine by me," I yelled.

"I feel like a leopard-woman in these pants!" Her voice grew fainter as she hurtled toward the elevator. "You think Mr. Corlis would have a heart attack if I growled at him—in a friendly kind of way?"

The apartment shrank a little after she'd gone. I finished dressing, reloaded the Magnum, and tucked it into the shoulder harness. I called the office and Fran's cool efficient voice assured me that nothing exciting had happened, and she frankly doubted it ever would. I told her if a guy named Julie Kern should call in the afternoon, to make sure and get a number where I could call him back, and I probably wouldn't get into the office at all today.

Then I called the Sutton Place penthouse, and after a while, a cautious voice answered.

"Danny Boyd," I said.

"I'm glad to hear your voice, D. Boyd, after the dreadful happenings of last night," Osman Bey's petulant voice answered. "I was worried for you after you left."

"Julie Kern told you about the agreement we figured out?"

"It gladdened my heart! So clever and so logical, D. Boyd!"

"Fine," I said. "There are a couple of small points I'd like to check with you, Mr. Bey, and they are kind of urgent. Okay if I come right over?"

"Now?" He didn't sound enthusiastic.

"Be there in fifteen minutes," I said, and hung up quickly before he could argue.

I picked up a cab five minutes later. Outside the temperature was already hovering around ninety, with the limp humidity that only Manhattan can breed. Through the park, only the kids had any vitality left, and even the squirrels moved listlessly like they'd only just learned the tragic news that human nuts weren't edible.

This time, the Sutton Place penthouse door opened within a couple of seconds of my first ring on the doorbell. It was only the first of a whole series of radical changes. The second was the fully dressed slave girl who opened the door to me.

"Oh," Selina said in a brooding, sullen voice. "It's you!"

She wore a gaily colored cotton print that slid all over her statuesque curves in ecstatic abandon every time she moved. Only it didn't match the dark circles under her eyes, or the painful, stiff-legged walk, as she led the way into the living room.

"Selina?" I said. "You look like you just got back from a professional wrestling tour and you never won a fall, even. What happened?"

She turned her head, and her brown eyes smoldered malignantly as she glared at me. "It's all your fault!" she said venomously. "Last night, I figured Julie was set to make you a permanent write-off. Then the next thing I knew he came back here talking like you and him were old buddies from way back! He said he offered you the chance of having me delivered to your apartment, so you could even up the score for the way I pretended you hurt me real bad last night, and you refused. 'That Boyd,' Julie said, 'he don't like to bruise a dame, but it's all the same to me.' Then he went on with a lot of junk about how I'd gotten out of line and needed a lesson!"

"I'm sorry," I said.

"You're sorry!" she snarled. "In a couple of places I won't even mention, even my bruises have got bruises!"

By that time we'd reached the center of the living room and I stopped and looked around. It hadn't changed any—the shades still pulled tight so the room was in semidarkness, that aromatic smell of burning incense, the hookah. Osman Bey himself sat cross-legged on a plush cushion, looking just as repulsive as ever.

"Greetings, D. Boyd!" He smiled up at me. "How can I help you this morning?"

I tried to remember the very first time I saw him, and what my first reactions had been.

"Selina," I said. "Would you help Mr. Bey onto his feet for a moment?"

"If it is necessary, I can stand!" Osman Bey said with great dignity, then heaved himself clumsily onto his feet.

One of those first impressions floated back into his mind. His beard had looked like an afterthought with the glue peeling—and he'd looked like an unnamed disease.

"Now, D. Boyd?" he said almost angrily. "Why do I have to stand in front of you like some low-born servant?"

"Last night," I said, "when I gave you a detailed run-down on what had happened to me over the last twenty-four hours, I told you Frankie Lomax was convinced that somebody named Corlis had sent me into his club, and you said, 'Corlis, who is this Corlis?' Remember?"

"Why would I not remember?" he snapped. "It was a logical question, I'd never heard of the man before!"

"He owns a fine arts gallery on Second Avenue," I said bleakly. "He's been buying from you for years—I've even seen your accounts in his office."

"Ah!" He struck his forehead a resounding blow the flat of his hand. "*That* Corlis!"

"That Corlis," I said, "but not *this* Osman Bey."

Maybe the first time the beard had been a genuine afterthought with the glue peeling. This time it was far more securely fixed to his chin, and he yelped painfully as I ripped it off. I grabbed a handful of long black oily hair, and suddenly found I'd scalped him. The removal of the toupee revealed a bristling gray crew cut underneath.

"I guess you can explain this, Mr. Murad?" I snarled "Only it had better be good!"

"All right," he said crisply.

His hands disappeared beneath the blue silk shirt and fumbled for a few moments until the bulging paunch disappeared, and an inflated rubber cushion bounced onto the floor. His fingers worked gently inside his mouth until the fat cheeks were hollow again once the rubber pads were removed. His back straightened to a ramrod stiffness and the metamorphosis was complete. Osman Bey had vanished, and in his place stood his partner, Abdul Murad.

"I am truly sorry for deceiving you, Mr. Boyd," he said with fierce dignity. "I pray you will accept my profound and humblest apologies!"

"Convince me you had good reason for it, and I'll accept your apologies with pleasure, Mr. Murad," I said flatly. "If you don't convince me I'm going to beat the hell out of you right here."

"I had no choice," he said quietly. "You already know a lot of the story, Boyd. For years Osman Bey had been using our legitimate business as a cloak for his smuggling activities. It is maybe ironic that I stumbled on it, when he wrote asking me to obtain a rare first edition of *Fénelon* for him personally, and suggested perhaps my daughter, Marta, could bring it with her on her forthcoming visit to New York. He even gave me the name of the bookshop which had the first edition for sale, and suggested what price I should pay for it!

"So it was done. The man in the bookshop insisted

NYMPH TO THE SLAUGHTER 103

he should package the book himself, so if it should be accidentally dropped on board an aircraft, from a car, no damage could be done to the binding. Marta took it with her when she left Paris on the plane for New York. The same day a man in my own organization was discovered tampering with a consignment of legitimate pieces of Kurdistan pottery which had great value as genuine antiques. He was packing the vases very ingeniously with foreign currency."

Abdul Murad's dark eyes burned fiercely for a moment. "I interrogated the man myself before I turned him over to the police. He confessed everything, and it was then I realized for the first time that Osman Bey had been fooling me for years. I called him long distance and told him he had exactly twenty-four hours before I place evidence of his guilt before the American authorities. He whined and pleaded until finally I hung up on him."

His jaw tightened suddenly. "Then six hours later he called *me* long distance. Marta had arrived safely in New York, he said, but then had been kidnaped. She would come to no harm just so long as I withheld that evidence from the American authorities. Once he and I had reached some written agreement on this matter, he felt sure she would be released!"

"He didn't even mention the first edition?" I queried.

"Oh, yes, he mentioned it!" Murad smiled grimly. "Where was it, he demanded to know? I told him Marta had it with her when she boarded the plane in Paris and that was all I knew. From there, when my former employee's confession had implicated the bookseller, it wasn't hard to trace back until I found the man who owned the diamonds and wished them transported illegally into New York—Big Max Morel, as you know.

"I went to see him—he already knew the diamonds had disappeared and was very angry. I put my cards on the table—I wanted my daughter back, he wanted his diamonds—why shouldn't we help each other? He told me to contact Julie Kern, his right-hand man here, on arrival and he would give me all the help he could.

"I got here the day following Marta's kidnaping but didn't dare reveal myself as Abdul Murad, naturally. Kern told me about Lomax, who was convinced Osman Bey had somehow cheated him, and had Bey prisoner somewhere in his own club. But whatever Lomax did to him, Bey still swore he knew nothing of the diamonds. So then I conceived the idea of impersonating Osman Bey himself—of hiring a private detective to help find my daughter—you, Mr. Boyd."

"And somebody got into Lomax's cellar and killed Osman Bey the night before last," I said. "Why?"

Murad shrugged. "I do not understand the working of these American criminals' minds, Mr. Boyd, I'm afraid. I can see no logical motive for killing Bey at all!"

"And still nobody apparently has ever seen the diamonds—or the book either, I guess?" I said.

"No." He smiled faintly. "If my daughter was not so vitally involved in this affair, Mr. Boyd, frankly I should worry more about the book—it is a magnificent translation. Yusuf Kamil Pasha is one of the immortal names in the history of our literature."

"Well," I said hopefully. "Maybe we'll get lucky and find both. Do you know where you can contact Julie Kern right now?"

"Yes."

"I think we should set up a meeting for, say, a couple of hours from now. Julie, yourself, me, and Lomax. There's only one place your daughter can be, and that's the Corlis house out on Long Island, but we have to figure out how to get inside the place first!"

"I'll call him now," he snapped.

After Murad had left the room, Selina looked at me with a mocking smile on her face. "So you finally figured it out for yourself, big brain! After you'd gone last night with Julie, me and Abdul had hysterics all over again about the big act we put on when you busted in here! 'May you spend eternity sitting on a

NYMPH TO THE SLAUGHTER

sharp pole'—" She suddenly dissolved into helpless laughter.

"You remember I figured you as having been planted real close to Osman Bey, by Julie?" I asked, when her laughter had subsided into an occasional helpless gurgle.

"Sure," she agreed. "You were right, but you had the wrong Osman Bey."

"But all the time you were with the real Osman Bey, you never found out about his close association with Beatrice Corlis?"

"No." She looked at me with sudden suspicion. "Why?"

"It only proves Bey was smarter than you thought," I said. "He knew you were a plant by Julie, but I guess he figured it was worth it. You don't get a belly dancer, built the way you're built, for free very often, right, Selina?"

"You—" she said bitterly.

"I'll make you a deal," I told her. "You stop laughing at me and I won't start laughing at you."

We sat around the table in the penthouse dining room, Julie facing me, and Abdul Murad facing Lomax.

"Okay, Danny," Julie said in an almost pleasant voice. "This is mainly your idea—so go ahead."

"You mind if I get a couple of details straight in my own mind first?" I quiered.

"Why not?" he said with a shrug.

I looked at Lomax and saw the sullen hate staring back at me from his lifeless eyes, set under the beetling eyebrows.

"For a long time Osman Bey had brought in illegal merchandise for Beatrice Corlis," I said. "She had her husband's fine arts gallery as a legitimate cover, and she could move the stuff fast and with little risk. It was a good working arrangement for both Beatrice and Osman Bey. Then Mr. Murad dropped his thunderbolt, giving Bey twenty-four hours to run, before he turned over all the incriminating evidence to the American authorities. In a panic, Bey ran to his long-time associate Beatrice Corlis for help. I'll bet the idea of kidnaping Marta Murad to keep her father quiet, came from her?"

Lomax nodded silently.

"Frankie," I said easily. "I'm asking you all this, because you must have gotten it from Bey while you had him locked in your cellar, right?"

"Yeah," he said thinly. "That's right."

"So Beatrice sent a couple of her hoods to kidnap the girl at the hotel?"

"Right!" He nodded again. "But Bey swore that when he called the girl right after she checked in, she told him she knew nothing about any book she was supposed to have with her!"

"The lying dog!" Murad said passionately. "I know he's dead, but even so—" He suddenly smashed his fist down onto the table violently.

"There was a choice," I said. "Either Bey had gotten hold of the diamonds and cached them some place and therefore was lying—or Beatrice's hoods had grabbed them along with the girl."

"No." Frankie shook his head firmly. "Bey knew Beatrice's hoods never found them—he talked with her before I grabbed him. She told him the girl swore she knew nothing about any diamonds either, so if you want a choice, Boyd, you got to choose between Bey and the girl. One of them was lying and, like you said, had already cached the diamonds some place."

"You're talking about my daughter," Murad said in an ugly voice. "I won't—"

"Save it!" Julie told him. "Danny's about to make a point, right?"

"The only real way to find out the truth would be to put the girl and Bey together," I said. "One would have to be telling the truth, while the other would have to be lying. That way you'd have to get the real truth eventually."

"I wanted to do that right from the start," Lomax

said bitterly. "But that Corlis dame was talking about a fifty per cent cut for herself! A crazy woman!"

"I got one question, Frankie," Julie said in a suddenly soft voice. "All the time you knew about the Corlis dame—you knew she had the girl! How come you never mentioned it to me?"

"Because I owed you, Julie," Lomax said bitterly. "I made the whole deal for you with Bey. You were holding me responsible for the diamonds or their cash value. I figured if I got them back, everything would be fine between us again. But if I told you about the Corlis dame and you got 'em back for yourself? Well—" he shrugged "—you'd spit every time we passed on the sidewalk!"

"Last night at the Corlis house," I said, "Beatrice figured I was one of Frankie's boys, the same way he figured I was one of her boys. She's offering a deal to put the girl and Bey together, on a fifty-fifty basis if you get the diamonds. I think Frankie should call her now and agree, set it up for tonight."

Lomax stared at me blankly. "Are you out of your mind, Boyd? Bey's been dead for over thirty-six hours, somebody got to him in my cellar, you know that! You and Leila found his body."

"Sure," I grunted. "I know it—the four of us know it—but Beatrice doesn't."

"Danny," Julie said softly, "you're thinking."

"But we still can't produce Bey tonight!" Lomax grated.

"You don't have to. You call Beatrice and say you want to come out to her house tonight and talk over the deal, and if it looks okay you can set it up for tomorrow night and bring Bey out to her place then."

"What happens if Frankie does go out there tonight?" Julie asked.

"I want you to go with him—Beatrice can't object, maybe she'll expect it. And if it's okay with you, Frankie, take Leila along with you."

"What the hell for?" he said furiously.

I explained the layout of Beatrice's house as I'd

seen it the night before. The ten-foot-high brick wall with the electrified wires on top of that—the impregnable gates operated by remote control—the five dogs—the four hoods, if Beatrice had been telling the truth; I'd only seen two.

"The kid, Michael," I said to Lomax, "he's skirt-crazy and Leila could keep him distracted all night. There's another thing, they won't let you or Julie into the place until they've collected your guns. Maybe Leila could get one in under her skirt, or someplace else?"

Lomax shrugged impatiently. "The whole idea's crazy!" he said in an openly contemptuous voice. "We get inside the place to talk about a deal we can never make anyway. Why do we bother?"

"Because while you're keeping them occupied inside the house, Mr. Murad and me will try and get in the other side, from the beach."

"What about those five dogs you're so scared of?" he sneered.

"I'm promised they'll be taken care of," I said, then told him about Matthew Corlis's message.

"You got to be out of your mind, Boyd!" The veins corded on Frankie's forehead as he shouted the words at me. "You're going to take a chance like that on the word of a little gutless creep like Corlis!"

"You could be right." I shrugged. "The way I see it, we don't have any choice."

"That's the way I see it," Julie whispered.

"I, too!" Murad said harshly.

"Okay—" Frankie shrugged helplessly. "You guys please yourselves. Me—I want no part of it."

"You got just one easy way out," Julie told him, the white scar at the corner of his mouth starting to vibrate slowly. "You give me the cash value of those diamonds—two hundred grand!—and you're out."

"Julie!" Lomax's face whitened. "You know I can't do that! I don't have that kind of money."

"Then you're in!" Kern said brutally.

Five minutes later the meeting broke up. Lomax

NYMPH TO THE SLAUGHTER 109

left immediately after having called Beatrice Corlis, who was delighted to set up a meeting for eight-thirty that night. Murad said he was tired and he'd get some rest, then went to his room.

Julie Kern still sat at the head of the table, his fingertips drumming restlessly.

"Danny?" he said finally in a low voice.

"Yeah?"

"Maybe there's another problem we got tonight we never talked about at the meeting."

"Like what?"

"While Frankie had Bey locked in that cellar, I went down with him three, four times," he said softly. "That Osman Bey had no guts at all—like he'd scream before you touched him, even! I made up my own mind he never saw those diamonds. So—if I'm right?"

"It has to be the girl?"

"All Murad wants from this deal is his daughter back," Julie whispered. "But before that, maybe we have to get to her a little, see what I mean?"

chapter 10

I called around four in the afternoon, and a blithe voice answered, "Matthew Corlis Fine Arts—Miss Torrence speaking."

"I was wondering," I said, carefully altering the pitch of my voice so she wouldn't recognize it, "if you could possibly help me locate a very rare print?"

"We'll certainly do our best, sir," she said dubiously. "What kind of print?"

"Leopard-skin," I said blandly. "Would you mind, Miss Torrence, taking a quick peek under your skirt, and see if it's still there?"

For a split second there was a dreadful silence, then she suddenly dissolved into laughter. "Danny Boyd! I'll get even for that, you see if I don't!"

"You didn't get fired after all?"

"No—" Her voice sobered suddenly. "Mr. Corlis didn't get in until after eleven himself, and then he only stayed an hour and went home again. Danny— I'm worried about him. That case you're working on— is he in bad trouble?"

"I think so," I said gently.

"I could feel it." Kitty's voice was tinged with sadness. "Oh! He gave me another message for you!"

NYMPH TO THE SLAUGHTER

"What did he say?"

"He said, 'Tell your Mr. Boyd that what I do for him I do gladly with no strings. But conceivably there may come a time when I shall expect a small favor and I trust that he will grant it.' It sounds awfully solemn, Danny, doesn't it?"

"Yeah," I said blankly. "I am also the bringer of lousy tidings, honey."

"Like what?" she said quickly.

"Tonight. I'm going to be busy."

"Oh, hell!" she said bitterly. "All night?"

"I wish I knew," I said fervently. "If there was any possible way I could duck out, I'd—"

"I know," she said softly. "I got the feeling this is the final night in whatever it is you're doing, from the way Mr. Corlis acted. It's tough, and I'll bleed and cry a little, and all the spots on my leopard-skin pants will turn white overnight, and—hey, Danny?"

"Yeah?"

"Would it be okay if I went over to your place tonight, anyway? Then if whatever it is does end earlier—"

"I think that's a wonderful idea!"

"Good! Don't do anything stupid like let yourself get shot at, or anything?"

"Are you kidding?" I asked in a horror-struck voice. "And risk getting the profile chipped?"

I went back to the apartment and had a couple of hours' sleep, then took a shower and got dressed in a dark shirt and an old pair of dark pants, then put on a pair of black sneakers. The harness fit under a dark sports coat and I shoved a handful of spare slugs in one of the pockets. I remembered the flashlight when I left around seven, and grabbed a quick meal before I picked up Abdul Murad in Sutton Place.

Julie Kern, Frankie Lomax, and Leila Zenta were due at the house at eight-thirty, and they wouldn't leave before ten whatever happened. I aimed to have Murad and myself on the beach by nine. I didn't want us climbing the cliff face while it was still light and we could be spotted from any point above, and I didn't want us climbing it in the dark, either. There wasn't only the climb to contend with, according to Corlis's information; there were trip-wires, too. So dusk was the compromise.

We made the beach by nine, and the thunderheads piling up across the Sound made the remaining light a hell of a lot less than I'd expected. It didn't make the cliff face looming over our heads look any more encouraging, either.

"Those clouds are going to get worse," I told Murad. "I think we should start up there right away."

"I agree," he said. "Have you much experience in climbing, Mr. Boyd?"

"Not until tonight," I admitted.

"I have done some climbing in Switzerland," he said. "May I suggest I go first?"

"With pleasure," I said sincerely. "Watch out for the trip-wires when you get close the top, huh?"

For the first hundred feet or so, it wasn't too bad. There were places where you could walk a few feet, and even the steeper slopes meant more a scramble than an actual climb. But after that the going suddenly got a lot tougher. I was more grateful than Murad would ever know to have him ahead of me, picking his handholds and toeholds with methodical care, then pointing them out to me afterwards. Maybe three-quarters of the way up, I made the mistake of looking back to see how far we'd come. For a paralyzing moment, the near-dark void that seemed to open up an inch below my feet swam in a dizzy whirl, and I leaned frantically against the cliff face, my fingers scrabbling at bare rock, until everything was still again.

Twenty feet from the top, and the cliff face was perpendicular. I got real obstinate then and refused to think about it. The darkness seemed to close in suddenly with no warning at all—my whole existence narrowed down to the handholds that had been Murad's toeholds, and would eventually become my toeholds, too. I'd almost gotten used to my tiny world, when Mu-

NYMPH TO THE SLAUGHTER 113

rad suddenly disappeared. One moment he was right there maybe six feet above me and the next moment he'd vanished.

What the hell had happened to him, I wondered frantically. He couldn't have fallen, I would have heard him, or seen him plunge past me on the way down. The nerve ends at the base of my neck began to creep. A giant bird? What did they call it—a condor? That was something out of science-fiction by way of South America, circa 1920. Ridiculous! So what happened to Murad? A giant bird yet! If it's so funny why can't I laugh?

"Murad!" I said in a piercing whisper. "Where are you?"

His head loomed suddenly two feet above mine, but *facing* me.

"What the hell are you doing?" I moaned in anguish. "Going back down the hard way?"

The idiot thought that was funny and chuckled softly.

"I wouldn't want to interrupt your fun," I said bitterly. "But I'm stuck right here and my fingers are starting to cramp! Are there any special birdcalls you want me to make on the way down?"

"Mr. Boyd!" His voice was suddenly concerned. "I thought you knew?"

"What?" I snarled.

"You're exactly six inches below the top of the cliff. Just reach up with one hand, then—"

A few seconds later I stretched out beside him on the grass and swore a solemn oath the next time I'd take a helicopter or the hell with it.

We rested for five minutes, and I checked my watch before we moved again, and saw it was nine-thirty.

"With your permission, Mr. Boyd," Murad whispered, "I will go first until we are level with the kennels, then I ask you to lead the way. And we crawl because of the trip-wires."

It was just as well we did crawl. Murad found three trip-wires in a line, each one about six feet behind the other. The first was six inches off the ground, the second eighteen inches, and the last one was real sneaky, just three inches off the ground. Finally we came level with the kennels and we climbed onto our feet.

"Now, I follow you, Mr. Boyd," Murad whispered politely.

The house, some fifty feet away, was a blaze of light. I wondered how the rest of them were getting on inside, and how Beatrice liked the competition of Leila Zenta for the kid's attentions. About ten feet back from the kennels, I heard a slow, ominous growl from inside. At least Corlis had managed to keep them inside the kennels and not running loose around the grounds.

By the time we reached the door, the whole five of them were growling steadily. It made for an interesting thought—were they penned up inside the kennels, or running loose? I had to fight hard to keep down my naturally chivalrous instincts, really force myself not to invite Murad to go first.

The door was closed, but not locked. With the Magnum clenched firmly in my right hand, I pushed the door open with my left. No slavering jaws slashed toward my jugular vein, so I figured it was reasonable to assume the dogs were penned in back of that reinforced wire mesh—the world was suddenly a happier place.

Murad followed me in and carefully closed the door behind him. I used my flashlight cautiously to show him the solid concrete floor.

"Tino—Beatrice's top hood I guess—said their half of the deal was underneath that floor," I told him. "There's about six inches thickness of reinforced concrete there. You think he was kidding?"

Without a word, Murad went down on his hands and knees and, while I held the flashlight for him, diligently searched every square foot of the floor. After maybe five minutes he suddenly grunted, "Here!" His finger traced a thin line in the concrete, until he'd outlined a rectangle about six feet by three. Then he

NYMPH TO THE SLAUGHTER 115

straightened up again slowly. "A trap door, Mr. Boyd. It must be operated by some remote-control device."

I shone the flashlight around the walls hopefully and came up with a big fat zero. The only projection I'd seen on any wall was a steel coat-hook at the far end, away from the dog pens.

"Nothing!" Murad said in frustrated fury. "If they are lying, if they have already—"

"Hold it!" I hissed at him. "I just had a hot flash from Matthew Corlis!"

He stared at me blankly. "What are you saying?"

"Part of his message," I said. " 'Find someplace to hang your coat!' "

I almost ran to the far wall, grabbed the steel hook, and pulled hard. It came away from the wall slowly like a lever, and there was a faint rumbling sound of well-oiled machinery. A couple of seconds later, the six-by-three concrete slab swung downward on counter-balanced hinges, leaving a gaping hole in the center of the floor.

Murad reached the edge of the hole about the same time I did, but while I stopped and shone my flashlight into it, seeing the concrete floor some five feet below, he dropped down into it and landed heavily on his heels.

"There is a passageway and I can see a light," he said eagerly, craning his neck to look up at me. "I shall investigate."

"Sure," I said. "I'll watch things here."

He disappeared from my sight, and there was nothing I could do but wait. At the other end of the kennels, the dogs padded up and down continously, snuffling and whining, bumping the mesh with enough force to make me wince most times it happened.

Then from the direction in which Murad had disappeared some ten seconds before, came the most horrible sound I had ever heard. It was a scream, deafening in its intensity, and terrifying in its agony. A sound that beat against your eardrums in a blend of horror and grief and guilt until it became unbearable, so you had to fight the impulse to turn and run with both hands pressed hard against your ears to blot out the soul-destroying intensity of it.

I did the last thing I wanted to, dropped down into the hole and landed heavily on the concrete floor below, the way Murad had done. I ran in the same direction he had taken, and saw a light ahead of me. The narrow passageway opened out into a cell-like rectangular room. There was a door at the far end, and a trestle bed placed against the longer wall.

Murad stood beside the bed, his head thrown back while the unendurable sound of his emotional agony gushed from his throat. A dark-haired girl lay face down on the bed, her naked body completely still. I went over and took a closer look. There were livid weals raised from her flesh in a seemingly unending pattern of horror, running from her shoulders down to her calves. I went to turn her over and her flesh was icy-cold to my touch. Finally I managed to turn her onto her side.

She still held a clumsy metal spoon clenched tight in the rigid fingers of her right hand. The handle had been worn down—by how much primitive rubbing I didn't dare think—to a sharp point. By deliberately falling forward onto it she had managed to plunge the point into her heart. But not by falling onto the bed with a canvas frame! Someone had been here after she died and lifted her back onto the bed. There were heavy bloodstains, some still not dry, in the opposite corner of the room.

Marta Murad must have been a very pretty girl, I thought dully, while she was alive. She couldn't have been any more than twenty years old. What kind of monster was responsible for the weals that formed a demoniac pattern almost covering one half of her body? What kind of beast could give a young girl the determination to spend all the laborious hours rubbing that handle to a sharp point? What kind of fiend could make her so sure that death was infinitely preferable to further suffering?

NYMPH TO THE SLAUGHTER

From some place above the trap door I could hear people shouting and running, but it didn't seem important. Murad hadn't moved from the exact position he'd been in when I entered the cell-like room. His head was still thrown back, the veins knotted in his neck, only now his vocal chords had dried out. Somehow the silent screaming seemed worse than the sound.

I shouted at him and he didn't hear me, I tugged his arm and he didn't feel it. After a little while I gave up; I wasn't sure if anyone could communicate with him then and I was even less sure whether they had the right.

By the time I reached the open trap door again, the overhead light from the kennel ceiling flooded the whole area with harsh white light. I looked up at a ring of faces that stared back at me dumbly in some ritualistic rite of shared horror. Nobody moved to help me out, so I had to wrestle my way over one edge, inch by inch, until I had enough leverage to pull the rest of my body clear.

When I got onto my feet and turned toward them, they still stared dumbly, as if they had an instinctive feeling that so long as the silence was unbroken they couldn't be forced to share whatever horror lay below the floor.

I stared at each one of them in turn. Julie Kern, his cruel face composed and expressionless; Frankie Lomax, much too taut and maybe starting to crack under the strain; Leila Zenta, shaking uncontrollably, going to pieces so fast you could almost see it happening; Beatrice Corlis, her complexion a little paler than usual and just a faint crack in her hard-lacquered eyes; Tino, like Julie Kern, waiting, watchful; Michael, his face gray, his mouth working all the time; and finally Matthew Corlis watching me with a steady gaze for the first time since I'd known him.

"Mr. Boyd," he said quietly. "What has happened down there?"

"The girl is dead," I told him. Then I described

how she had died, and maybe why, from the physical evidence I'd seen.

A few seconds after I'd finished, the sound of slow, dragging footsteps came from the underground passageway. Then Abdul Murad came into sight, walking like a man suffering an intolerable burden. When he got to the trap door I offered my hand to pull him up and he ignored it. He placed the flat of his hands on the floor—which was level with his chin—then pulled himself out of the hole in a smooth, incredibly powerful movement that brought his hips level with the floor so it was easy to swing one leg across.

He stood up and looked at them all with an expressionless face for maybe ten long seconds, then spoke in a hoarse whispering voice that still sounded like a scream.

"My daughter," he said. "Which of you is responsible for what happened to her?"

"Beatrice?" Julie said easily, after another long silence. "Who was in the house all the time you had the girl a prisoner down there?"

Her eyes flashed their hatred toward him, then she spoke in a slightly shrill voice. "I don't understand how it could have happened! Unless, somehow, some monster stumbled on the secret of the switch and—"

"After that first day," Tino said suddenly. "I watched him in the mornings and the evenings and we turned off the power to the machinery at night. I kept the key hidden, always. But the afternoons—" He stared at her bleakly. "The afternoons," he repeated slowly, "he spent with you."

"Always!" Beatrice nodded like a marionette. "Every afternoon—with me!"

"My dear?" Matthew Corlis said in a voice that sounded gentle but wasn't at all. "Don't I remember some bargains being made? Be a good boy, Micky, and be nice to your Queen Bee, and you can have that suit you like so much?"

"Well!" The lacquer suddenly split and fell away, and the things revealed in her eyes were unspeakable.

NYMPH TO THE SLAUGHTER 119

"Yes, I suppose we used to play silly games like that sometimes, but Micky never—"

"Sometimes"—Matthew sounded like he was making idle conversation—"sometimes you would make the bargains, my dear, and sometimes he would make the bargains?"

"Oh, yes, of course." Her head jerked forward eagerly. "It was such fun for the two of us!"

"And how you must have hated yourself for not having the guts to stand up to her, eh, Michael?" Matthew said blandly. "A woman thirty years older than yourself—and a dirty, vicious-minded woman at that!"

"Yeah!" The kid nodded jerkily. "Some nights I'd lie awake until it was light, making plans to kill her. Only she was the boss and maybe I wouldn't ever have it so good again—you know how it is?"

"It gets to a point where you have to work it off somehow, or your brain will just explode," Corlis said gravely.

"You got it!" The kid's face was suddenly animated. "But the deals you got to make! All the time, deals! 'Look,' I'd tell her, 'I'll make you a real great bargain. Tomorrow afternoon I'll do whatever you want—whatever you say—no arguments! Just give me an hour this afternoon alone with that stinking little witch who figures she's too good for me and I'll—I'll—'"

"I thought you did," Corlis said simply.

The kid backed away with terror-stricken eyes as Murad took the gun from his pocket and raised it slowly. The gun fired three times, and as the last two slugs hit, the kid's body flopped across the floor in a convulsive reflex.

Leila fainted and slid onto the floor at Lomax's feet, and he didn't even notice. Murad lowered his gun for a moment, then turned stiffly toward Beatrice. She saw it in his eyes and screamed thinly, then ran toward her husband in a grotesque waddling motion that was slower than a walk.

"Matthew!" Her face contorted with the passionate will to live. "Matthew, save me!"

"Save you, my dear?" He laughed suddenly with genuine amusement. "Whatever for?"

She thrust him out of her way with one flailing arm and tried for the door. Murad waited patiently until she reached it, then fired two more shots. Her wide back arched in agony, while her massive arms still flailed the air in a hopeless effort to drive her forward to safety, then she fell backward and hit the floor with a shuddering crash. Her head came to rest pillowed awkwardly on Michael's chest.

Murad looked down at the two of them, smiled vaguely, then thrust the barrel of his gun hard against the roof of his mouth and pulled the trigger.

"Poor bastard!" Tino said in sudden compassion as he looked down at him.

"You want to cry for somebody, cry for his daughter, Tino, not him," I said.

"How's that, Boyd?" Lomax said sharply.

"There was a whole lot of guilt mixed up with his grief, Frankie."

"How do you mean—guilt?" he snapped.

"When he hired me he pretended he was Osman Bey and wanted me to find his partner's daughter who'd been kidnaped, and the missing diamonds, too. The one lead he could give me was an old girl friend, Leila Zenta. Did anybody tip you off I was coming that night, Frankie?"

"Yeah," he said, nodding slowly. "Maybe fifteen minutes before you showed up, some guy called me and said I should stay close to Leila because a real mean hood was on his way to see her."

"He conned you," I said slowly. "He conned me and he conned Julie."

"How's that again about me being conned, Danny?" Julie asked softly.

"What did he tell you, Julie?" I asked. "That he was the one guy in the whole world who could get any information out of Bey easier than blowing a whistle? But he couldn't approach Frankie, because maybe Frankie knew who had his daughter and it

NYMPH TO THE SLAUGHTER 121

could harm her if they knew he was in New York?"

"Strictly one hundred per cent, pal!" Julie admitted grudgingly. "Let's hear the rest."

"You'd been down to the cellar with Frankie enough times to memorize the combination and pass it onto Murad. The two of you followed me to the club and once you saw me make my move, you tipped off Frankie. Then a little time later Julie walked in on us to make sure we were kept there long enough for Murad to have time enough to question Osman Bey.

"And Murad goes straight down to the cellar, murders Bey, and walks straight out again."

"It was an accident, he told me!" Julie snarled. "He got carried away, the knife slipped!"

"Julie," I said feelingly, "There are times when you're downright naive!"

"What's with that crack, Boyd?" he whispered.

"Think about what kind of a motive Murad could have for killing Bey."

"I don't get it!" he said coldly.

"You remember Murad's story about how he stumbled onto what Osman Bey had been doing for years —using his company's legitimate exports as a cover for smuggling?"

"Sure, I do!"

"That rare book with the diamonds hidden in the binding? Just imagine for a moment if everything happened the way Murad said it did, only it all happened a couple of days earlier?"

"You flipped, or something, Boyd?" Lomax asked blankly.

"Say he catches his employee stuffing currency into those vases on Monday, and finds out what Bey's been doing all these years. Then on Tuesday he gets the book Bey's asked him to send across with his daughter who leaves Thursday. Murad's a fan of the guy who translated the book a couple of centuries back, so he takes a good look at it. Then he remembers what he's found out about Bey and takes an extra good look—

and comes up with diamonds worth a couple of hundred grand."

I took a deep breath. "What can he lose? He's about to give Bey twenty-four hours to run before he tips off the American authorities—and when the people who consigned the diamonds start looking for the fall guy, Bey is the obvious choice."

"You mean, then it went wrong for him?" Julie said. "When they kidnaped his daughter?"

"Sure. Because Murad was the only one who knew for sure that the diamonds had never left Paris. Once Frankie had gotten together with Beatrice on a deal to find out who was telling the truth, the chances are they'd believe Bey a lot easier than they would his daughter. So he couldn't let that happen—the only sure way to stop it was to murder Bey."

"So we don't got no diamonds?" Julie said thinly. "We never did have them, right?"

"Right!" I said.

He looked down at Murad's body almost at his feet and his white scar started to throb deeply. "You lousy bum!" he said bitterly. "When I think I gave you Selina—for free!"

Within the next quarter-hour they had all gone, except for Matthew Corlis and myself.

"This might prove difficult for you, Mr. Boyd?" he said quietly. "For your license, I mean?"

"It will," I said bleakly. "Not reporting Bey's body —not reporting a kidnaping, consorting with about every known hoodlum there is, it feels like, anyway!"

"Why did you do it?"

"I figured as long as there was a chance of the girl being still alive, the rest of it didn't matter too much," I told him honestly.

He nodded slowly. "I think you were right. We know Bey was murdered by Murad, and now he also is dead. I think you should go now, Mr. Boyd."

"I'll stay and wait for the police," I grunted.

"It would be most stupid!" he said coldly. "I am perfectly capable of doing that, and I also know the whole story." His mouth tightened slowly. "And I also share the guilt, which you do not!"

His logic was right. "I don't know how to thank you properly, Mr. Corlis," I told him.

"Why don't you get the hell—ah—out of here?" he suggested coldly.

I sneaked into the apartment a little after midnight without switching on any lights, then tippytoed across the darkened living room to the bedroom. I carefully inched the door open wide enough to poke my head around the frame. Life was suddenly lousy. Her cabin trunk was still there, but she wasn't. The bed looked cold and empty and repulsively uninviting. I thought, the hell with it, I'll get drunk.

"You sure this is your apartment?" an acid voice asked. "The way you sneak around it, the rent must be overdue."

There was a faint click and shaded table lamp cast its warm, inviting glow across the couch.

The conical hair-do was immaculate with not one blonde hair out of place. There was a grave, questioning look in the cobalt-blue eyes, and a serious expression adorned the elfin face.

"Is it all over?" she asked.

"All over," I agreed.

"How about my Mr. Corlis?"

"A nicer guy never walked this earth!"

"I'm glad!" She relaxed back into the couch and I could only see the top half of her head.

"I'm afraid you don't have a job any more," I said gently.

"Didn't I tell you, Danny?" she said airily. "I made a deal with Mr. Corlis this morning. I bought the gallery."

"You what?"

"I guess I never did mention that Daddy's stinking rich," she said, very casually. "Made all his money out of teeth."

"He's a dental surgeon?"

"No—" she yawned gently. "Bubble gum manufacturer."

"You're putting me on!" I said murderously.

"I swear!" She lifted her right arm negligently. "Give me an honest answer, Danny Boyd. Are you afraid of me?"

"You're out of your mind!"

"Then why don't you get a little nearer? It's like talking to someone in the next apartment right now."

"Sure," I said happily. "Here I come."

Her eyes watched me with a grave intent as I cut down the distance between me and the couch.

"I whipped us up a batch of drinks," she said nonchalantly.

"Great! Like what?"

"I don't have a name for it yet," she volunteered, after a slight hesitation. "And I got a new outfit today."

I came around the end of the couch like a homing pigeon, then stopped dead.

"You approve?" she said, smiling hopefully.

"I just don't see it," I gurgled.

"Oh, that. Well—" That dangerous lower lip protruded another quarter-inch. "I was scared it might get crushed while I was just sitting around, so I took it off. But I can easily put it back on, if you like?"

"No," I said slowly, "I don't think so."

"Somehow," she said demurely, "I didn't think you would."

Other SIGNET Mysteries You'll Enjoy

DEATH ON LOCATION   **by William R. Cox**

Murder stalks a carefree movie set on location in Las Vegas. (#S2158—35¢)

DON'T JUST STAND THERE, DO SOMEONE
                                               by Don Von Elsner

A scheming beauty queen takes suave lawyer, David Danning, for a ride that leads straight to blackmail and murder. (#S2134—35¢)

THE KILROY GAMBIT   **by Irwin R. Blacker**

A top-secret Washington agency has to battle meddling congressmen and enemy agents to accomplish its mission of Cold War espionage. (#S2063—35¢)

A VERY PRIVATE ISLAND   **by Z. Z. Smith**

This taut story of a man trapped on an island with a killer is top-drawer suspense right up to its dramatic finish. (#D2186—50¢)

THIS MAN DAWSON   **by Henry E. Helseth**

Colonel Dawson of the Metropolitan Police matches his steel-trap mind against the lethal cunning of a notorious crime king. (#S2109—35¢)

THUNDERBALL   **by Ian Fleming**

Secret Agent James Bond meets the blackmailing challenge of a mysterious organization which has highjacked an atomic bomb. (#D2126—50¢)

GOLDFINGER   **by Ian Fleming**

James Bond thwarts an evil genius who has worked out a fool-proof plan to rob Fort Knox. (#D2052—50¢)

THE CONFESSION OF ALMA QUARTIER
                                               by David Robinson

The shocking affairs of a beautiful socialite whose promiscuity leads to murder. (#S2103—35¢)

THE PRAYING MANTISES   **by Hubert Monteilhet**

Distinguished as the best mystery novel of the year in both France and America. "A lethally potent cocktail." *Anthony Boucher*.   (#D2308—50¢)

THE CRUMPLED CUP   **by Henry Kane**

A teen-age "Lolita" has a rendezvous with death on a deserted beach.   (#G2301—40¢)

THE DECEIVERS   **by Richard Goldhurst**

A wounded veteran, transformed by plastic surgery, becomes an impostor and discovers a crime no one had suspected.   (#S1958—35¢)

CLIMATE OF VIOLENCE   **by Russell O'Neil**

A frank, disturbing novel about teen-agers who take part in a gang rape, and the shattering effects on their lives.   (#T2188—75¢)

THE SPY WHO LOVED ME   **by Ian Fleming**

For the first time, secret agent James Bond is seen through the eyes of a passionate woman in this tale of high-tension in the Adirondacks.   (#D2280—50¢)

TWILIGHT OF HONOR   **by Al Dewlen**

This taut drama of a vicious murder and a sensational courtroom trial was a Book-of-the-Month Club selection in its hardcover edition, and winner of the McGraw-Hill Fiction Award.   (#T2257—75¢)

THE KILROY GAMBIT   **by Irwin R. Blacker**

A top-secret Washington agency has to battle meddling congressmen and enemy agents to accomplish its mission of Cold War espionage.   (#S2063—35¢)

THE MANCHURIAN CANDIDATE   **by Richard Condon**

A Korean War hero is brain-washed and becomes an assassin against his will. A movie starring Frank Sinatra, Laurence Harvey, Janet Leigh and Angela Lansbury.   (#T1826—75¢)

FATAL STEP   **by Wade Miller**

>A hard-boiled private eye stalks a cold-blooded gunman through the tawdry glitter and eerie shadows of an amusement park. (#S1911—35¢)

A KISS BEFORE DYING   **by Ira Levin**

>A superb thriller about a vicious young man determined to murder the girl who loves him. (#S1770—35¢)

A TASTE FOR BLOOD   **by John B. West**

>In this fast-paced bout with mayhem and murder, private eye Rocky Steele is enmeshed in a dope racket controlled by ruthless and cruel killers. (#S1800—35¢)

DEATH ON THE ROCKS   **by John B. West**

>Rocky Steele, on vacation in Africa, gets involved with a blistering babe and a deadly diamond. (#S1883—35¢)

JUST NOT MAKING MAYHEM LIKE THEY USED TO
                                                          by Don Von Elsner

>The second of the Colonel David Danning mysteries, in which the brilliant sleuth tests his mettle against the mastermind behind a cruel extortion racket. (#S2040—35¢)

BULLETS ARE MY BUSINESS   **by John B. West**

>Rocky Steele slams through another tough thriller, gambling on odds in a bout with murder. (#S1852—35¢)

THOSE WHO PREY TOGETHER SLAY TOGETHER
                                                          by Don Von Elsner

>The first in a fascinating mystery series featuring Colonel Danning, a new kind of private sleuth who associates with Board chairmen, big time stock manipulators, and powerful con men. (#S1943—35¢)

To Our Readers: If your dealer does not have the Signet and Mentor books you want, you may order them by mail, enclosing the list price plus 5¢ a copy to cover mailing. If you would like our free catalog, please request it by postcard. The New American Library of World Literature, Inc., P.O. Box 2310, Grand Central Station, New York 17, New York.

THE BEST READING AT REASONABLE PRICES

signet paperbacks

SIGNET BOOKS *Leading bestsellers, ranging from fine novels, plays, and short stories to the best entertainment in the fields of mysteries, westerns, popular biography and autobiography, as well as timely non-fiction and humor. Among Signet's outstanding authors are winners of the Nobel and Pulitzer Prizes, the National Book Award, the Anisfield-Wolf award, and many other honors.*

SIGNET SCIENCE LIBRARY *Basic introductions to the various fields of science — astronomy, physics, biology, anthropology, mathematics, and others—for the general reader who wants to keep up with today's scientific miracles. Among the authors are Irving Adler, Isaac Asimov, and Ashley Montagu.*

SIGNET REFERENCE AND SIGNET KEY BOOKS *A dazzling array of dictionaries, thesauri, self-taught languages, and other practical handbooks for the home library, including nature guides, guides to colleges, bridge, job-hunting, marital success, and other personal and family interests, hobbies, and problems.*

SIGNET CLASSICS *The most praised new imprint in paperbound publishing, presenting masterworks by writers of the calibre of Mark Twain, Sinclair Lewis, Dickens, Hardy, Hawthorne, Thoreau, Conrad, Tolstoy, Chekhov, Voltaire, George Orwell, and many, many others, beautifully printed and bound, with handsome covers. Each volume includes commentary by a noted scholar or critic, and a selected bibliography.*